Senior Snoops

An Agnes Barton Mystery

Madison Johns

I DEDICATE THIS BOOK TO THE FEISTY AGING POPULATION THAT NEVER GIVES UP THEIR THIRST FOR LIFE.

Edited by Arlene R. O'Neil
Cover makeover by http://www.coverkicks.com/
Re-edited by
Proofreader Cindy Tahse
http://www.smashingedits.com

Also By Madison Johns

Coffin tales Season of death
Agnes Barton Senior Sleuths Box Set Books 1-3
Armed and outrageous (Book 1)
Grannies, guns and ghosts (Book 2)
Trouble in Tawas (Book 4)
Treasure in Tawas (Book 5)
Pretty, Hip & Dead (Agnes Barton/Kimberly Steele Cozy Mystery
Pretty and Pregnant
Redneck Romance

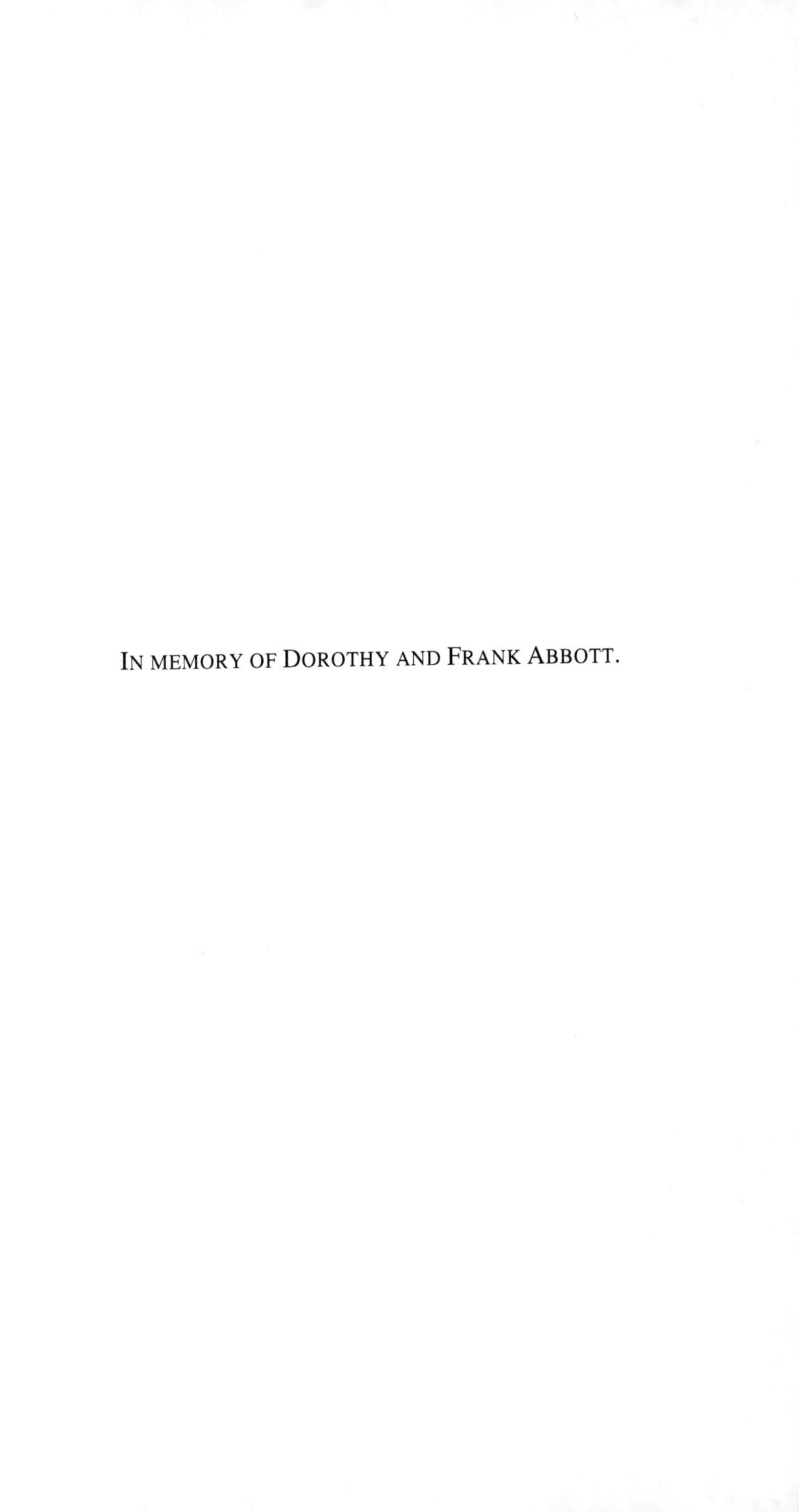

In memory of Dorothy and Frank Abbott.

Chapter One

I adjusted the waistband of my khaki crop pants and smoothed my bright aqua shirt into place. As I slid my feet into white sandals, I yelled, "Eleanor Mason! If you don't hurry, we're never gonna make our flight."

Eleanor, with string bikini in one hand and tanning lotion in the other, said, "Hold onto your granny panties. I'll be ready soon enough."

I raised one brow. "This year or next?"

With a huff, she turned and mooned me, and then continued to shove items into her oversized suitcase, including her denture cup and Efferdent. "I'm glad that we're going to Florida for the winter."

"And why is that? Besides the obvious sunshine and no snow, that is?"

"Buff men on the beach can't hurt either."

"Eleanor," I gushed in mock disapproval. "You're eighty-two, dear."

"Yes, and I'm not dead yet." She ginned widely. "And try not to act so innocent, Agnes Barton. I know what goes on in that Winnebago of yours when Andrew Hart visits."

"We-Well, I-I … That's none of your concern."

Eleanor batted her eyelashes. "I guess it doesn't matter that you're seventy-two either, dear."

"Nope," I laughed. "I guess not. We older gals need some lovin', too. But what about Mr. Wilson? Is he coming to Florida with us?"

"I'm really not sure yet. How about your hot shot lawyer man, Andrew?"

I sighed. "He said, 'I'll meet you there when I can'."

"Why, for a retired lawyer he sure works a lot."

"I know. I really should say something about that."

Eleanor and I are senior snoops or private investigators. The main difference is that we don't charge a cent for our services. I giggled. I don't think most folks care to have us on a case … if they're a bad guy or gal, that is. After our last case, Sheriff Peterson promised us a trip to Florida. That case hadn't gone according to plan, but neither does any case we're on.

Plus-sized Eleanor was crammed into purple capris and tee. She didn't much care what people thought of how she dressed or how many rolls were displayed. I hardly think she cared much about anything except for snooping out clues with me. Well that … and Mr. Wilson. He's the man she's been getting busy with. It's a running joke that we still don't know Mr. Wilson's first name and that he doesn't remember it either. I, on the other hand, have a red hot romance going on with the lawyer, Andrew Hart.

I frowned as Eleanor climbed atop her over loaded suitcase and sat on it; I'm guessing in an attempt at closing it enough to zip, although how she had planned to do that while sitting on it, I wasn't sure. She wobbled a bit and toppled to the floor.

"A-Are you okay?" I hid a smile with my hand.

"The least you could do, Aggie, is not laugh until you know I'm okay."

Tears ran down my cheeks. "I-I'm sorry, but it was so funny. First you were balancing yourself on the suitcase and then boom, you hit the floor."

"I'm happy to be part of your entertainment. Are you planning to help me up or what?"

I helped her up like she helped me whenever I found myself in a jam. "Hurry, or we'll never make it to the landing strip."

"Landing strip?" Eleanor asked. "You make it sound like we're going on a small plane."

"I'm not sure, but Sheriff Peterson lined us up with a charter flight from the Iosco County Airport."

Eleanor's face turned white. "Then it's probably a one-way ticket."

I laughed. "Come on, El. Peterson has changed his ways."

She put her hands up. "I'm okay with it if you are. Florida for the winter sounds yummy."

"Yummy?"

"Yes," she giggled, "As in man eye candy yummy."

My hand went to my hips. "I thought you and Mr. Wilson were exclusive."

"We are, but it doesn't hurt to look," El said in mock shock. "It's not like I'd cheat on the old boy, but I'm old, not dead."

I decided to let this topic drop. I hauled the suitcases through the house and outside where Sheriff Peterson awaited us. He was using his squad car to take us to the airport. "I don't suppose you can go back in and carry the rest of the suitcases?"

His face darkened and then he burst into a fit of laughter. "Of course, Agnes." He rushed into the house carrying them happily to the car and loaded them inside.

Once Eleanor and I were sitting in back of the squad car, we roared up the road. Eleanor grabbed ahold of the metal cage separating the front seat from the backseat and screamed. "Slow down. You're speeding!"

"Yup, I am. I'd hate for you two to miss your flight." He paused. "If it makes you feel better, I'll turn on the sirens." He flipped a switch and my ears rang as the sirens blazed to life. Cars pulled over to the side of the road, and when I glanced at Eleanor, she had a huge smile plastered on her face.

"This is exciting," she said. "I always wanted to be in a police car chasing bad guys."

"Maybe we should get a siren for your Caddy then, dear."

"That's a great idea, Agnes. I'd be lost without you."

"It's against the law. Unless you're a cop, that is," Peterson reminded her.

"Fun sucker," Eleanor retorted.

"She meant that in a nice way, Peterson," I added. I nudged Eleanor and whispered into her ear. "Knock it off before he hauls us back home and we're stuck here for the winter."

As Peterson drove along a curve, Lake Huron was visible. The lake was calm today as was the wind, but it was only September. Soon, the temperatures would drop and snow would come.

I'd miss East Tawas, Michigan, and hoped no crime sprees would happen while I was away. I mean, what would the sheriff do without El and me chasing down clues?

Peterson made the turn into the Iosco County Airport and I gasped when I saw how tiny the airport was. Okay, so I know East Tawas is a tourist area, but really, couldn't they at least have a bigger airport in the county? Even the closed Air Force base in neighboring Oscoda would make a larger airport.

I suppose that not many people fly into Iosco County to visit the Lake Huron shoreline. It sure is a beautiful drive on US 23. It's scenic with a great view, but many closed down businesses. US 23 had a slew of thriving gift shops and such, but now they primarily are in East Tawas and Oscoda.

I smiled when I spotted the Cessna Citation II/SP on the runway. At least we would be traveling in style, but still. "How long is that runway? It hardly looks long enough for the plane to take off."

Peterson sighed. "It's 4,802 feet long, plenty long enough for a safe take off. Unless." he paused.

"Unless what!" I shouted.

"Unless a seagull hits the plane," he laughed. "That only happened once and nobody was injured. I promise I'll be on the lookout until you're safely in the air."

El wrung her hands. "That plane looks too small. Are we the only ones that will be on board?"

Peterson clammed up and I wondered what gives, until I noticed Dorothy and Frank Alton standing outside with suitcases! Dorothy was Eleanor's nemesis. I just shook my head; this wasn't going to go well.

When the squad car screeched to a stop, Peterson opened the door for us and quickly retrieved our suitcases from the trunk. “He seems almost a little to eager for us to leave,” El pointed out.”

“I see that, El, but the truth is I’m kinda happy about leaving myself.” I waved at Dorothy and Frank, and gave El a pinch when her eyes bugged out. “Behave,” I whispered to her. “I have never been to Florida and I’m more than happy to leave Michigan behind for the winter. How about you?”

She began to spout off. “Why is Dorothy here? No way do I want to be stuck in a flying tube with the likes of her.”

I sighed. “I know how you feel, but she’s not that bad. She has been out of town for awhile; maybe she’s changed.”

“Some cats just can’t change their spots,” she pouted. “She’s a bully.”

“Maybe she wouldn’t be if you’d quit hitting on her husband.”

Eleanor smiled at that. “I only do that because it annoys her.”

“But you have Mr. Wilson now.” I searched the airport and then asked, “Is he going to be here or not?”

Just then, a state police cruiser came around the building and stopped. Trooper Sales ran around and opened the door for Mr. Wilson, helping him out and handing him his walker. Mr. Wilson’s walker had wheels on it, but they were smaller so that it didn’t move too fast. His rail-thin body was clothed in gray Dockers with a matching gray shirt, white sneakers on his feet. Obviously, Mr. Wilson hadn’t changed his style of dress since before he retired.

From under a fishing hat, Mr. Wilson greeted us.

"Oh, sweet Eleanor. I'm so glad the trooper whisked me here before the plane left."

"Me too, hun." She rushed over and gave him a peck on his gaunt cheek.

Trooper Sales yanked Wilson's suitcases and helped Sheriff Peterson to load them onto the plane. They ended up loading everyone's suitcases. "Thanks, Sales."

Trooper Sales was a good trooper with a huge heart. He wore his dress blues today and his shoes had quite a shine to them. His black hair even looked freshly cut. I wondered where he was going today. *Stop it, Agnes.*

I kept staring at Sales until he finally said, "Sophia wanted to be here, but she's sick today. Your daughter, Martha, will be here soon. She didn't want you going to Florida solo."

I was betting Martha wanted a free trip to Florida, too. We had been at odds for years, but she turned up in town not long ago, and we'd been trying to mend our relationship. Sophia is my granddaughter. I was more than a tad disappointed she wasn't coming to Florida, but then again, she works at the hospital as a nurse. I imagine that it's hard to get time off. She also has been dating Trooper Sales, which I'm still trying to swallow. In my book, nobody is good enough for my Sophia.

Rocks tumbled forward as Martha's station wagon came into view. She jumped out and adjusted her hip-hugger jeans. Her midriff top with the words "Wild and Crazy" was knotted at her waist. She clickety-clacked across the asphalt and stood near us, waving at the occupant of her car, who promptly whirled the station wagon around and drove off, a smoke trail in its wake.

"I can come, can't I?" Martha asked, biting a fingernail. "You said—"

"I told you that El and I were going to Florida, if memory serves me." I darted a glance toward Peterson. "I hope it's okay."

"Of course. The pilot is a friend of mine and he's flying to Florida, so the more the merrier."

I could tell Martha relaxed at that by the way she dropped her shoulders. She fluffed her wild blond hair with the too-much hairspray and smiled. "Thanks, Clem." She winked at Peterson.

The door to the Cessna opened and a man appeared dressed in pilot whites. "Come on board, and welcome." He was of medium build with a goatee, which he thoughtfully stroked.

Mr. Wilson moved his walker forward and was helped inside first. We all followed suit except for Eleanor, who got on last. She bit her lip nervously as she made way between the narrow seats and sat in the one next to me. "It sure is a tight squeeze," Eleanor said.

"Oh, my! I swear I felt the airplane drop when Eleanor came in," Dorothy Alton said snidely.

"You'll feel your bottom lip fall if you say another word, Dorothy," I reminded her. "No need to be nasty." I thought speaking on Eleanor's behalf this time wouldn't hurt. As it was, El had her hand balled into a fist and was rubbing it suggestively while glancing Dorothy's way.

Dorothy shouted, "She was looking at my Frank!"

Frank slapped a hand over his bald head. "Here we go again."

Martha turned and glared at Dorothy. "If you don't want to come on this flight you can catch another."

Good for Martha, I thought.

Dorothy opened her mouth for a hasty retort, no doubt, but then shut it with a gnashing of teeth. It was like nails on a chalkboard.

I gave Martha a nod as she sat next to Mr. Wilson. Looking at El, I said, "Why aren't you sitting next to Mr. Wilson?"

"Because I wanted to sit by you is why. I'm too old to be wrapped around a man twenty-four seven." She said it like someone in her forties and not a woman of eighty-plus.

"Okay, but you know Martha is gonna be flirting with him. It's what she does."

"I know, but ultimately she always ends up with a man half her age. It's just what happens," she giggled.

I knew Eleanor was right. The truth was that I didn't know who Martha was anymore. Since she showed up in town, things have been mighty interesting. Her daughter, Sophia, had pushed her off on me, and truth be known, I wasn't too happy about it. But I was determined to make the best of it and roll with the punches. I frowned; I sure hoped Sophia was okay. I pulled out my cell and dialed her number. She answered on the first ring. "Are you okay, honey? If you want, I'll postpone my trip to Florida."

She squealed, "Don't you dare. I'm fine. Bill is here and he'll look after me. If I feel better soon, I'll meet up with you."

"Oh, don't put yourself out. I can't imagine you want to hang out with us old folks in Florida anyway."

She giggled and then ended the call with a barfing sound. I clicked off the call and told Eleanor what she said.

"So, Trooper Sales is looking after her, eh?"

"Yes. They're dating now, remember?"

El gazed down at her freshly painted fingernails that were fuchsia in color, and then back at me. "She's sick, like with the flu?"

"I suppose so. Poor thing was barfing when I hung up. Why?"

"Do you think it's the flu or something else altogether?"

I narrowed my eyes. "I don't know what you're hinting at here, but get it out of your mind. I won't stand for any more assumptions about my granddaughter. Got it?"

"Fine," Eleanor said holding up her hands. "I won't say that she might be p—"

"You said you'd drop it."

"I never said anything like that, but I'll drop it if you like." She smiled sheepishly. "Trooper Sales is a great guy and will do the right thing by her, don't worry."

I turned my back to her and stared out the window. Outside, Sheriff Peterson was talking to the pilot and handed him a suspicious looking envelope. How much had it cost to send us packing and how badly did Peterson want to get rid of us? I knew the answer. Quite a bit I imagined, but that was fine with me. El and I had been a thorn in his side for a while now. He wasn't that happy we kept butting into his cases, but what's a body supposed to do when crime comes knocking in your town? So whatever the reasons, it was nice he paid for the trip. He even had accommodations for us.

"What gives out the window?" El asked.

"Oh, nothing. Just glad we're getting out of town for the winter, is all."

"Who needs all the snow when we can go surfing?"

"Did you rattle something loose, dear? Neither of us is young enough to risk a broken bone."

"Speak for yourself. Eighty is the new twenty I hear."

"Forty, tops."

"What does that make me?" Martha asked from her seat.

"Sixteen," El said belly laughing. "So, young lady, you better start behaving."

"No way! I'm going to be rebellious. Maybe if I did that when I was younger, I'd be more settled now."

I nodded. "I'll give you that much, Martha. You were a good girl. I never worried for a minute about you."

The pilot came on board and told us to fasten our seat belts, reminding us the plane was smaller so we'd feel the turns. He showed us all the safety equipment on board, pointing out the oxygen masks. I laughed it off, of course. I mean, what could happen, right?

The Cessna roared to life and we taxied down the runway. I bit down on my lip when I saw how short the runway really was, and a white tail deer appeared.

"Deer on the runway!" I screamed. I gripped the arms of the seat and we glided above the deer without a problem. I could clearly see the deer's white tail as he sprang away. Poor thing was probably having a heart attack. "Is everyone okay?" I asked. They all laughed at my antics.

"It sure was nice of that white tail deer to send us off, don't you think, Aggie?"

"I could have done without it."

"Aw. It was nice to see you come unglued for a change. It's usually me."

I bit my lip as we made the first of the turns the pilot told us about, and gasped as we flew over Lake Huron. The sky was clear and blue and the lake calm. It was a welcomed sight, but a sad departure. I hadn't ever been out of the state of Michigan and it made me a tad nervous. Hopefully, Peterson put us up in a nice place far from the busy cities that I was sure dominated the state. But then again, how would I know since I had never been there?

Chapter Two

When Lake Huron dropped from view, I settled back into my seat. “Help yourselves to a beverage,” the captain said over the loud speaker. I stood up, making my way toward the front of the plane and spotted a refrigerator that contained both pop, which was a Michigan term for soda, as well as beer. I raised a brow, but grabbed Diet Coke for everyone.

“I want a beer,” Martha said. “I saw beer in the refrigerator,” she pointed out.

“Serve yourself then, dear, but try to behave yourself if that is at all possible.” I knew it wasn’t. Martha was bad enough when sober.

She sauntered over to the fridge, bent at the waist, and retrieved a beer. A wolf whistle split the air and I glared at Mr. Wilson, but then heard, “Frank, how could you!”

“Oh stop it, old woman,” was the reply. “If you did that, I’d whistle at you, too.”

I bit my lip to stifle a laugh, but Eleanor didn’t. “Yeah, Dorothy, live a little.”

Dorothy’s face reddened. “I-I know how to have fun.”

“Playing video poker doesn’t count,” chimed Frank. “How about a little wrestling?” he winked.

“How about if we change the subject?” I suggested. I couldn’t handle the image in my mind of the two of them together in that way and neither could Dorothy by the way she clammed up and faced the window.

"Are we there yet?" Eleanor asked with a smile.

"You might as well take a nap, El, because it will be a long time before we get there. I imagine we'll have to gas up somewhere along the way, too."

"I have plenty of gas," Mr. Wilson said, and then tooted.

I closed my eyes. I might as well take my own advice. Besides, the view outside my window wasn't all that good anymore, just tiny specs and squares of property that could only be viewed from up above. "Buckle up, everyone," I suggested.

***

I was jolted awake as the plane skidded on another runway. When my eyes snapped open, we were at a small airport and the plane moved toward a filling station. The pilot waved as he left. "This shouldn't take long."

We stayed on board, but my eyes were peeled to the pavement as two men in dark suits approached the pilot. After a brief exchange, one man searched him.

Unsatisfied, the other man shot the pilot. He glanced toward the plane and right into my ever-watchful eyes. Details started to run through my mind. He was a large man with a hawk-like nose and piercing brown eyes. I undid my seatbelt and ran over and shut the door.

"What's going on?" El shouted.

"I think we're being hijacked!" I fired back.

Frank Alton slapped his seatbelt aside and said, "Bullshit!" He made his way to the cockpit of the plane.

My whole body was trembling. "Wh-What are you doing?"

"I'm flying us out of here," he said with confidence.

"Oh, Frank," mouthed Dorothy. "You can barely drive a car anymore."

My eyes snapped back to Frank. "Do you have any flight experience?"

"I was in the Air Force."

I would have said more, but the sound of gunshots out the plane's doors made me follow Frank to the cockpit. We sat, buckled up and I nervously watched as Frank guided the airplane down the runway, snapping off the hosing that connected the plane to the gas pump. Soon the airplane taxied down the runway and as Frank pulled back on the handles, we roared into the air. I called the police and they gave us a direct line to the nearest airport and directed us there, promising the police would meet us.

I thought about calling Sheriff Peterson, but this wasn't his jurisdiction. I found the packet that Sheriff Peterson had given the pilot and it was filled with cash! My eyes widened when I counted out twenty-five thousand dollars, all in hundred dollar bills. What was the sheriff up to this time? I thought to hold the money for a while, but the police would want it for evidence. Decisions, decisions.

Thirty minutes later we flew over an airport that had sirens and flashers of emergency vehicles near the runway. "Yipee," Frank said as he glided the airplane down the runway and braked, but we were going too fast and the plane swung sideways. Screams pierced my ears, which unnerved me when I realized they were my own.

"Hold on to your asses," Frank cussed. Smoke filled the air and I panicked. Were we on fire? Suddenly the plane came to a stop and I sat there a few minutes before I could move or even breathe, it seemed.

On shaky legs, I stood and helped the occupants from the plane, and down the steps that led to the tarmac below. Mr. Wilson was handed his walker and he rolled it forward to a formidable group of police officers.

Two men in brown pants and white shirts with black ties led us inside and into an interrogation room that consisted of only a long table and chairs surrounding it. We sat, and a man pressed his palms on the table. "Out for a little joy ride, were you?"

"No, it was no joy, I assure you." I slapped back a strand of my salt and pepper hair. "We were about to be hijacked. I told somebody that when I called it in."

The two men snickered. "Highly unlikely."

I puffed up my chest. "What did you say your names were?"

The men exchanged a glance between them. "I'm Adam Putner." He thumbed in the other man's direction. "This is Clyde Palmer. We are from Homeland Security."

My eyes narrowed. "Are we under arrest, Putner?"

"No, but I'd like to ask you a few questions."

I took in a breath and searched the group of seniors to make sure they were okay. "Where's my daughter?" I asked.

"She's being strip searched."

My eyes narrowed. "Why?"

He ignored my question. "Do you know what the pilot was hauling?"

"Us, as far as I know."

"Did you find any packets aboard?"

No way was I telling them I had a packet tucked in my purse. "No, why? What are you looking for?"

"We're not sure yet, but it's illegal to haul drugs into another state."

Dorothy stood and said, "We need our medication."

"Is that all I'll find in your luggage?" Putner pressed.

I leaned back in my chair. "No, you might find some Preparation H, if that's what you mean. You can borrow it if you like."

"I have condoms in mine," El confessed.

Ignoring El, Putner remarked, "Such a smart mouth for someone in so much trouble."

"You said you just wanted to question us," I reminded him. "Are you done yet?"

"We really need to find that packet. Are you sure you haven't seen it."

"She just told you block heads she hasn't seen it," El said, huffing and puffing. "We don't need to take this kind of abuse. We're upstanding citizens of East Tawas, Michigan."

"And great investigators," Mr. Wilson pointed out.

I gulped at that. I sure wished he hadn't said that. "Yes," I stood and slapped my palms on the table. "So what gives? Back in the airport, the pilot was pistol whipped and then shot. I saw it all."

"Did you find his bullet-riddled body?" El asked with menacing intent.

"See? That's just the thing. We went out to the airport you stopped at and there was no sign of anything. No dead body or spent cartridges," Putner said.

I gasped. "Th-That's impossible. Are you sure you went to the right airport?"

"We tracked your plane, and lucky for you, we didn't shoot you out of the air!" Putner's brow shot up. "You must be mistaken, Mistress Snoopy Pants." His face reddened and I thought he was nearly ready to explode. "Why don't you just enjoy the winter in Florida like most of the old folks and don't cause any more trouble."

"Why, I never!" I shouted, but then calmed down when handcuffs were slapped on the table. "Okay, maybe you have a point."

"Aggie!" El shouted. "Are you going to let them talk to you that way?"

"Yes, I guess I am," I laughed nervously. "I don't care to spend the night in jail. Maybe you're right, but whoever they were, they shot at the plane. Did you happen to check for bullet holes?"

"Yeah," El cut in. "Did you?"

"We'll check into your story, but let us handle it."

"Fiddlesticks," El said.

Putner waved his hands into the air. "Get me away from these people before I go ballistic."

"Too late," I sung.

He glared at me and Palmer took his place. "Do you know anyone in Florida?"

I shook my head and smiled when I saw Martha enter the room. With a wink in Putner's direction, she sat.

Palmer eyed the group. "How about anyone else?"

Dorothy Alton raised a hand. "I think I can speak for the group and say no. Can we leave now?" she whined.

Palmer made way for the door. "Welcome to Florida, ladies. We'll be in touch. Just fill out the paperwork and you're free to leave."

We scrawled out our addresses in Michigan and then walked outside and retrieved our luggage, which was sitting in the waiting room. I phoned Sheriff Peterson and gave him a brief account and he told me that he'd have someone pick us up at the airport.

Chapter Three

We all fell asleep in the lobby and woke up as a man cleared his throat. When my eyes snapped open, it was to a man standing over me who wore a tan uniform with a sheriff's badge. He was tall at nearly six foot, and quite fit. His black hair was plastered to his head, most likely from the sheriff's hat that he held in his hands. "Hello, folks. I'm here to pick you up. The name's Calvin Peterson."

"Peter what?" El said. "You mean as in Peterson, you say?"

I shook my head in disbelief. "As in related to Sheriff Peterson?"

He beamed. "One and the same," he chuckled. "And I'm so happy to have you here in my home state of Florida."

I smiled at him, but my mind raced. Of all the dirty tricks.

El grinned and sidled up against Calvin. "You seem so much nicer than your brother."

"Bahaha," he snorted as he laughed. "I hear that all the time." His cheeks were rosy. "Seriously, though, there will be no snooping on my watch. Got it?"

I shrugged. "I'll try, but you know how we old ladies are."

"We're snoopy to the core," El cut in.

"Just my luck. My jail has plenty of vacancies."

My jaw slacked open as did El's. "Are you escorting us to the hotel?"

"Hotel?" he laughed. "Bahaha." He paused and then became serious. "You mean, my brother didn't tell you?"

"Tell us what," I demanded.

"Oh." He glanced away and when he locked eyes with mine, I knew in an instant that something was afoot. What did Peterson have up his sleeve?

With a wave of his hand, he instructed, "Follow me, ladies."

When he was out of hearing range, I spoke up. "Somehow, I think we just got a screw job."

"A what?" El asked, shaking Mr. Wilson awake.

"Peterson set us up," I spat. "I'm almost afraid to see the place he booked for us."

We assembled our group and pushed the cart with our luggage piled on it out the door, following the sheriff to a mini bus with the words, "Sunny Brooke Retirement Village" emblazoned on the side.

"What the heck!" I yelled. "I'm not going to any retirement village to stay."

Peterson smiled. "Well, no. You'll be working there for the winter. You don't think my brother has enough money to pay for a hotel, do you?."

"I'm not working there," Dorothy said nudging Frank. "Tell him, Frank."

"What about Mr. Wilson? How is he going to work? He can barely walk," El said.

I smiled widely. "If he can get freaky then—"

"Mom, TMI!" Martha said with her hands over her ears. "I'm sure it will be okay. They won't have you working twenty-four seven. There will be plenty of time for snooping on your off time."

"Eh?" Peterson started. "I said, no snooping on my watch."

"Then don't look," El stuck out her tongue.

"You don't live there too, do you?" I asked. When he shook his head, I added, "Okay, then, we'll deal. But I can't promise you how this will go."

Calvin gave the driver instructions and told us he'd follow us to the retirement village. With a wave of his hand, he was gone.

The ride to the retirement village was a bumpy one and with each rut, we bounced off our seats. The bus had ten seats side-by-side with an empty space in the back with straps where wheelchairs could be secured. From the way the driver drove the bus, he either didn't care much for senior citizens or he needed us at the village real quick. I didn't get that close a look at the man, but I'll definitely say my piece on my way out.

A halfhour later, we passed a large white sign with the words, "Turtle Dune Beach" scrawled across it in bold italics with an illustration of a turtle near the bottom of the billboard. The streets were lined with gift shops, restaurants, and candy shops, not much different from back home in East Tawas. We stopped at a light and a throng of people carrying surfboards crossed the walkway.

"Look, Aggie," El said. "You can almost see the beach down that street."

I stared down the crowded street and could vaguely see the blue water. I breathed deeply of the candy aroma. "Yup, and something smells yummy."

"Fresh fudge, hopefully," El's eyes danced. "Or a hot dog. I'm hungry."

"Oh, driver," I said. "Could you please pull over? We're hungry." He either didn't hear me or was ignoring me, so I got up and walked to the front of the bus.

"Get back to your seat, lady, or you're gonna get hurt." The man looked up into the mirror and I noticed his narrow eyes and sucked-in face with nearly a day's worth of razor stubble. I met his eyes. "Is that a threat or a heavily veiled request?"

He screeched to a stop. "I can't risk any of you getting hurt."

"Good to know. Now kindly open the bus doors so we can get something to eat."

"Yes, we're hungry," El echoed from the back of the bus.

From between clenched teeth he informed us, "You can eat at Sunny Brooke."

"Maybe I don't want to. Maybe I want to eat now."

"It's a free country," El chimed, her cheeks reddening in anger. "Open up or I will!"

The man stood up and obviously was attempting to stop us, but El rushed forward and pushed him down on the seat like a linebacker. She moved the lever that opened the door and we all exited the bus. I stayed behind to help Mr. Wilson, who needed his walker. Once we were outside, I gasped at the sights. When we crossed the street I spotted the sheriff's squad car. "Hurry. Here comes the fuzz!" I shouted.

We darted away, as fast as people of a certain age could go, and we disappeared down the street, hopefully undetected by the sheriff. Mr. Wilson wolf-whistled at the women who passed wearing only skimpy bikinis. My eyes widened, too. It was like Sodom and Gomorrah to us folks from up north. Even though we lived in a beach community ourselves, the women never wore bikinis that skimpy.

We followed the street and wandered into a candy shop, shoving in chocolate samples much to the chagrin of a woman who lingered close by and rolled her eyes. It made me burning mad, so I went over to her. “Hello, Ma’am. Could you please direct us to a good restaurant close by, one that has good food?”

The woman, who was dressed in a one-piece swimsuit replied, “I don’t work here.” Her eyes shifted toward the cashier who came over, but I wasn’t having it. “I only asked where was a good place to eat. What’s up with you? Besides that swimsuit up your crack, that is?”

Her face reddened as she called out. “Somebody better call Sunny Brooke. I think they have one of their escapees in town again,” she sneered.

I turned in time to see the Sunny Brooke bus coasting by the shop, in the same direction the woman had been looking. Otherwise, we could be any senior citizens in town for the winter.

“That’s awful presumptuous of you,” Dorothy said. “Sunny Brooke is just a retirement community, not a prison.” Her eyes darted toward me and I shrugged.

We wandered out and the cashier followed us. “Please don’t be offended. I’m Penny,” the girl began. She toyed with her apron that covered her red and white striped dress. “Last night one of the employees at Sunny Brooke went missing and I’m afraid it might be foul play.” She wrung her hands. “Ever since the robbery last week, folks are kinda on edge."

"Robbery?" El said with wide eyes. "Like in bank robbery?"

Confusion came over her features like she half expected us to know. "No, a jewelry store."

"Name, please. We need the name," El encouraged her.

"Julie's Jewels. It's down on South."

I glanced about to assure nobody was listening and asked, "What does that have to do with Sunny Brooke?"

She bit her lip. "Well, I-I." And just like that she clammed up.

"Please tell us. We're taking jobs there today," I said. "That is, unless you tell us something awful about the place."

"Well, all I know is that an employee there is missing and presumed dead."

My face tightened. "Why would they presume the person dead just because they are missing?"

She shrugged. "I don't know. I guess folks only think the worst. There was also another employee who disappeared and hasn't been seen since." Darting a glance inside, she continued. "The woman inside was just being snide. Please feel free to try another sample. I have chocolate caramel corn inside."

We wandered in and tried the samples, but somehow I wasn't feeling it. And it wasn't lost on me that Martha had disappeared. Not to worry, though. She's a grown woman and could take care of herself, I hoped. It occurred to me that I knew scant about my daughter's past. We had only reconnected a short time ago, and besides her being a bit on the wild side, I couldn't judge her. Lord knows, I had my moments.

"Aw, we're leaving, aren't we?" El asked.

"We might just have us a case at Sunny Brooke."

"What about the jewelry store robbery? Do you think there is a connection?"

I wiped my face with a napkin. "I'm not sure yet, but I sure as hell want to know." I paused. "And we'll never know unless we go to Sunny Brooke."

El wrung her hands. "She said it was an employee that was missing and it makes me nervous since we'll be working there, too."

"No need to worry, El. We'll stick together if you don't mind hanging out with Dorothy Alton."

"I guess I'll have to stomach the old bird, then. We can't very well let anything bad happen to her. Who else would I fight with?"

"That's what worries me, dear."

Chapter Four

We finally left with directions and ordered hot dogs from an outside vendor. Wandering back onto the main drag, I spotted police cruisers that passed us. I flagged one down, but before I could speak with the officer, Sheriff Peterson flew from down the street, his face beet red. "I told you—"

"No," I put a hand up. "I'm ... no, we're on vacation and I'm not allowing you to order me about. If you don't like it, we'll stay somewhere else."

He gritted his teeth. "You can't be commandeering the bus."

"In his dreams. We simply requested him to let us out. He was the one that got nasty," I informed Calvin. "We're ready to go to Sunny Brooke now."

He scratched his head. "You are? Is this some kind of trick?"

"Nope, please lead the way."

"Weren't there more of you earlier?"

"Yes, but we old folks tend to drop off without warning."

"I meant the younger lady."

"Lady?" El snickered. "You can't mean Martha. Why she's —"

"A free spirit. I'm sure she'll catch up eventually."

Calvin's eyes darkened, but he didn't utter another word. He led us toward the bus and I snickered when El stuck her tongue out at the driver as we boarded. We settled Mr. Wilson and he thanked me when I handed him his walker. "You girls sure like to shake it up," he said as he shimmied his frail body. "Just like an earthquake."

We enjoyed the rest of the ride until we saw the sign that read, "Sunny Brooke Retirement Village" in bold red letters. "Isn't red supposed to be a negative color?" El asked.

"I'm not sure, but since two employees went missing, one of them supposedly dead, it might be construed as negative."

"That makes me nervous. I sure hope we'll be okay there. I don't want to be a corpse." She grabbed my arm. "I'm too young to die!"

"There, there, no need to panic just yet. Besides, we're here now."

With a woosh and a gasp, the air brakes split the quiet that now overtook the bus. The lever was thrown over and we slowly moved out. El handled Mr. Wilson this time and once we were on solid ground, the door to the bus slammed shut. Obviously, the driver had had enough of us. If he'd at least been pleasant, I'd have felt guilty about how we treated him back in town.

I smiled when I saw the Mexican style exterior, the stucco walls leading all the way to the second floor and ending where the slate roof began. The property had palm trees in the front with a quaint, "Watch for alligators" sign. I laughed nervously. "I hope that sign is a joke."

"Well, we are in Florida, dear," El pointed out.

We stood there and waited until the sheriff's car

pulled into view and Calvin Peterson clamored out. It was kind of strange to refer to him as Sheriff Peterson after dealing with his brother, Clem, in East Tawas. Body-wise, he was nothing like him, but yet in actions, it was pretty much the same old thing; another sheriff who didn't want us butting in, which was one of the reasons I planned not to ask him too many questions, or else he'd be on to us like flies on honey. In my experience, the longer you can go without the law finding out what you are up to, it's all for the better. It's not like El and I made their job any harder, but from the way they acted, you'd imagine that they thought so.

Calvin pulled up his waistband at his approach and frowned at seeing the bus leave. "I promise I'll have your luggage here before tonight."

I raised a brow. "I sure hope so unless you're paying for it. It was you that insisted we come along, remember?" I meant to say more, but Eleanor interrupted my thoughts.

"Is the driver always so unfriendly?"

"No," Calvin said. "I guess you just bring that out in people. If you had just come straight here, none of this would have happened," he reminded us.

I rolled my eyes. "Are you leading the way inside or are we going to sit out here all night?"

He led the way, ignoring my question. Inside was a black and white tiled floor with a desk just inside the doors. Behind was a board posted with activities, such as shopping, movies, and dinner in town.

From behind us strode a woman wearing crème colored slacks that flowed over the high heels she wore as she clacked toward us. On her silky white blouse, she wore an oval pin with the name Bridgett Nelson etched on it. “I'm so glad that you're here and in one piece,” she began. “When Richard said you had left the bus in town, I-I was so worried.”

I stepped forward. “Richard?”

“Richard Cook, the bus driver, dear. You must be Agnes Barton. You look just like the picture Clem sent me via our last email. He told me that you're a great sleuth.”

I tried not to let that go straight to my head.

“Huh,” Eleanor spouted. “Earth to Aggie.” She then turned to Bridgett. “I'm Eleanor and—”

“You help her solve mysteries.” She clapped her hands. “We sure could use your help around here, then.”

We smiled, but our smiles quickly faded when she added, “I lost my earrings this morning and can't quite figure out where.”

“I see. Well, it beats me. I just got here.” There was something about this woman and her china doll features that I just didn't trust. She brushed a dark lock of hair from her face as she spoke, like every time! I was resisting the impulse to offer her a bobby pin.

I waited for her to say something, but she eyed Mr. Wilson. “I sure hope he can take care of himself. This isn't a nursing home,” she pointed out.

“Of course, dear. Don't worry about it a second longer. Right, El?”

El grinned. “Mr. Wilson is strong as an ox. He just needs the support of a walker, is all.”

Mr. Wilson nudged El. “That's my girl.”

“If you could kindly show us to our quarters,” I

said with a smile.

"Quarters?" El said. "As in like a hysterical romance?"

"I think you mean historical, dear," I hinted. "Nobody would believe anything ever written about us."

"True, but for some reason they buy every word Jessica Fletcher said in that television show, Murder She Wrote."

"I can't agree enough, El."

I stared at Bridgett who finally motioned us forward after a lengthy pause. "I'll show you where you can change."

"Change? Like into what?" El whispered to me.

And with a straight face I replied, "I imagine into a Wonder Woman costume, although I doubt I have the hips for it these days," I laughed.

We were led into a room with textured cream wallpaper and doors on corresponding sides. "Ladies to the right, gents to the left," Bridgett said.

"Party pooper," Mr. Wilson spouted as he rolled his way through one of the doors, followed by Frank Alton who shrugged.

Inside lockers were situated along one wall with a sink and door to the left. I guessed it must be the restroom. Dorothy opened a locker and gasped. I went to her side and stifled a chuckle when I saw the maid's uniforms. "I figured as much," I muttered and when Dorothy glared at me I added, "What did you expect? That we'd just be working the counter downstairs?"

"I didn't know, but Frank and I can find our own place. We have the money to spare, not like you two girls," she smiled.

El's head perked up at that. "Maybe we should ask Frank about it, then." El smacked her lips. "That is, if you'd ever let the poor man speak."

"Yeah. I mean ... on the airplane was the only time I ever heard him speak," I added.

Dorothy put her head down and admitted, "He doesn't hear all that well and his hearing aid doesn't help much."

"It would if he didn't have to turn it down to drown you out, Dorothy," El spat. "You have a great husband. You'd do yourself well to remember that."

"I do and you're right, Eleanor. I don't mean to be so nasty sometimes to you, but it seems like Frank likes you."

It was nice to see Dorothy and Eleanor getting along, but I knew it was a lull before the storm. I think their squabbles were what kept them both going most of the time. Although now with Mr. Wilson permanently in the picture, it might just change.

"Hug and get over with it already," I said eyeing the pair.

"Now, Agnes. I'm not so sure she wants to hug me," Eleanor said with her lips askew.

"Nonsense. I sure could use a hug after today," Dorothy said. "We're sort of on an adventure with you here."

El moved in ... Dorothy moved in — and they both had contorted expressions on their faces, but they hugged. I wouldn't call it a bear hug by any means, but it was a welcomed start. "I hope you two can keep the peace here. We have bigger fish to fry."

"Fish, but I'm not hungry now," Dorothy said. "We

just had a hot dog, remember?"

El smiled with a glint in her eye. "What my partner here means is that we have the perfect cover for our undercover operations."

Dorothy looked puzzled. "We do?"

"Yes," I grinned. "We can find out under what circumstances those two employees disappeared."

"I'm sorry, but you lost me."

"Remember back in the candy store the girl told us—"

"Eleanor Mason, I barely remember five minutes ago," she spat, tapping her foot.

"Let's just get changed and see what else Bridgett has in store for us."

Dorothy's eyes widened. "I'm not so sure I like the sound of that," she gulped. "I'll just play dumb, then."

El's lips turned up into a smile. "Which will be easy, because you're—"

"So smart, Dorothy. What a great idea." I nudged El in the ribs. "We should all play dumb, at least in front of Bridgett."

The door creaked open and Bridgett stood there with her arms folded across her chest.

I whispered, "We should hurry before Bridgett worries about what is taking us so long."

"And why would I worry with the likes of you ladies under the roof?" Bridgett asked with foot tapping.

El scoffed. "What in the heck is that supposed to mean?"

"I'm sure she meant it in a good way, not a bad way. Isn't that right, Bridgett?" I asked.

"Sure, whatever you say. But please get dressed or

the residents will be peeved their rooms weren't picked up." She closed the door with a thump, and if looks could kill, Eleanor would once again be guilty of a capital offense.

"Calm down, El. No sense in getting all worked up over a few words. Florida has a death penalty, don't forget."

El balled her hand into a fist and massaged it while going through lockers looking for a uniform that would fit. Finally, in the last locker, she found one. She pulled out a pink uniform with a large white apron that went over it. "Geez, this seems pretty fancy for a retirement village," she pointed out. "Somehow, I think we're in for a hard time."

Dorothy fidgeted. "I hope the residents aren't too particular."

I gave them a look that must have meant get dressed already, because they quickly donned their outfits and I followed suit. I did worry about our belongings though, but I placed them inside the lockers. With no pockets, I was forced to keep the pouch full of cash inside my purse.

"Are you ladies ready yet?" Bridgett inquired as she burst into the room.

"Yes, but I wonder about our belongings. I'd like to lock them up."

"Anything to get you old folks moving." She rummaged through a closet and came back with three locks. After we had our belongings locked up and the keys on a string around our necks, we followed Bridgett outside.

Chapter Five

Once we were in the hallway I squinted, my eyes searching for the men. "Where are Frank and Mr. Wilson?"

"Yes, where is my husband Frank, you hussy!" Dorothy spat.

Bridgett pursed her lips. "Calm yourself. I have them working in the kitchen."

"Frank can't cook. He doesn't even know where dishes or utensils are kept," Dorothy sighed.

Bridgett let out a breath. "I'm sure Darcy is showing them what to do, and we found Mr. Wilson a sit down job." She paused and then added, "If you please, ladies, I'll show you where the housekeeping carts are."

"Carts?" Dorothy asked nervously. "I thought we could do some team cleaning."

"You'll never get anything done that way. How about you each handle ten rooms a piece to start with?"

I put a finger in the air. "How many rooms are here?"

"About fifty, plus the restrooms in the commons area on both floors."

I frowned. "But that will take all day."

"Not if you hurry. Like I said before, the residents won't be happy if they return from lunch to a dirty room." She sashayed toward a room and pushed out cleaning carts, three of them, one for each of us. The large yellow cart had a trash bag insert and cleaning supplies. It also had a mop bucket that sat on a flat surface and a vacuum. "I suggest each of you start on a hallway with one of you starting upstairs."

"Are we the only cleaning ladies?" I asked.

After a lengthy pause she answered. "Y-Yes. That's all we have for now."

"I see. So how many employees do you have working here, besides us?"

"We can chat later, Agnes," she promised me. "But right now the rooms need attention." She handed us each a skeleton key, one that would open all the doors.

Clacking away with a scuff of her shoes, she disappeared into a closed room. "It's just a hunch, but I don't expect to get too much intel from her," I said.

Eleanor shuddered. "I like Dorothy's idea that we stick together. Who knows what we'll run into?" El said biting a finger. "I'd hate to see Dorothy go missing. With our history, I'd be the first suspect."

"Thanks, Eleanor. I think." Dorothy began. "I'd hate to run into any trouble without you girls," she smiled.

We started on the first floor and I saw that all the rooms had the same floor plan: a one bedroom with a modest sized living room painted all white with an equally white couch. I poked into the bedroom, which consisted of a full-sized bed with a mirrored dresser. Clothes were strewn across the room. I came back into the living room and we straightened magazines and newspapers, emptying the trash. We wiped down the bathroom, cleaned the mirrors, and vacuumed. After the first few apartments, we had it down to a system.

Eleanor vacuumed; Dorothy handled the trash and straightened things, leaving me to the bathrooms.

In the last room, Eleanor gasped. I walked from the bathroom to see what she found. Knowing El like I did, I just knew it meant something important. Dorothy Alton was trembling as she held a newspaper in her hand. "You might want to read this," Dorothy said with a screech in her voice.

I took the newspaper in my hands. There was a story about two missing workers at the Sunny Brooke Retirement Village. "Humph. It says here two maids disappeared and one has been confirmed dead." I gulped at that.

"I'm sure we have nothing to worry about, girls," Dorothy said.

"Well," Eleanor began. "Bridgett was trying to separate us."

"Still, if we are all they have for a maid service—"

"They'd want to keep us around," Dorothy interjected.

El rolled her eyes. "Good observation, and for once I'd have to agree with you, Dorothy."

Dorothy beamed, showing a mouthful of dentures that were too big for her small mouth, or so it seemed. I nodded at her. "We're going to be a great team."

"What?" Eleanor said with a full-on pout on her mouth. "Teams are two people, not three. Somebody is the odd duck."

"Oh, don't feel like that, Eleanor. I'm sure Agnes doesn't think of you like that."

I stifled a laugh. "Not to worry. This team of investigators needs all the help we can get."

"Does the newspaper say what they think happened to the maids?" Eleanor asked.

"It doesn't, but it does say they might have been attacked by an alligator from a nearby swamp." I strode to the window and walked out onto the patio where I saw an iron fence that bordered the property. Sure enough, there was a swamp out back.

El's eyes bulged. "Of all the places to build a retirement village."

"Maybe it's that swamp land people can buy on Craig's List."

"You must mean Ebay, dear. I don't think Craig's List sells property," Eleanor offered.

The damp mustiness clogged up my airway and I coughed, which didn't help much. My face and arms warmed quite nicely from the bright Florida sunshine. Thick green foliage hid any real view of the swamp.

After what seemed like ten minutes, I stated, "We need to check out the patio area." I slid open the patio doors and stepped on the beige tile. I whirled around and motioned the girls forward, but neither of them moved.

"W-We'll wait for you right here," Eleanor announced. "Isn't that right, Dorothy?"

Dorothy wrung her hands. "I-It might be dangerous."

"Oh, I thought you wanted to be part of my team. Just forget I asked."

That moved Dorothy into action. It was then that Eleanor moved outside, too. I just knew that would work. No way would Eleanor let Dorothy in on our investigating unless she was up to her knees in it herself.

With Dorothy along, it might be the best idea yet. If anything, she's a great motivator.

We trudged through the thick green grass that could have stood a good cutting. But who knew? Maybe it was too dangerous. Who knew what might be hiding in the tall grass? I froze when I heard a distinct rattling of sorts that I just knew wasn't any of us breathing. "I sure hope that isn't a—"

"Snake!" Eleanor screamed as she ran back toward the patio.

Dorothy shrugged and sidled up to me. "I-I'm not afraid. Are you?"

"Nope." I made my way toward where the iron fence bordered the property. There was a gate and I inspected it. It swung open with little effort. "That sure is odd. The gate isn't even locked."

"You're right, Agnes. Why, just about any kind of wildlife could wander inside."

I gulped. "Maybe we should join Eleanor on the patio," I shrieked and ran toward where I thought we came from, but it was hard to tell since Eleanor was nowhere to be found. "Oh, great!"

Just then, a patio door opened and Dorothy and I trekked there. Once we were inside, I raised a brow as a smiling man who looked to be about seventy greeted us wearing only a towel! His chiseled chest shone like he had just came out of the shower. "Thanks," I said.

Dorothy was eying his man parts, hidden from view.

"Dorothy, stop that. You're married."

She snickered. "And what might your name be?"

"I'm Eugene Bragsworth. You ladies shouldn't be

outside. There are alligators and snakes out there."

"I should have known better, but I wanted to check out the gate. It's not even locked!"

"Wouldn't surprise me." He went toward the bathroom. "I'll be back in a jiffy."

His towel flew out the door and both Dorothy and I stood, shell-shocked. This man was just as fit as Andrew, my love. It was a fine time for that man of mine to take off when he should be here with me.

Eugene appeared wearing tan shorts and a white tee with the words Crab Shack in large orange letters. He smoothed his grey hair back and asked, "Are you ladies new residents?"

"Nope. We're working here."

"Maid service," Dorothy added. "My husband, Frank, is working in the kitchen."

He bent low and took Dorothy's hand into his, kissing the back of it. "Your husband had best keep an eye on you, dear lady. You're a ray of sunshine."

"Oh, you go," Dorothy gushed.

Obviously he didn't know whom he was speaking about. Dorothy was anything but a ray of sunshine.

I frowned at Dorothy's antics. "I heard there were two maids that turned up missing here?"

Eugene swept one hand over his head. "It was just dreadful what happened to Mary Lou. She was a kind soul."

"What did happen?"

"Well, the gators got her for sure."

"How can you be certain?"

"Yeah," Dorothy interjected. "Did you see it first hand?"

"No, but we found her shoe near the swamp. That's proof enough, if you ask me."

My lips formed into a straight line. "Not quite, but I can see why one would believe it was the gators."

He scoffed at that. "What are you trying to say, exactly?"

"Well, to be blunt, I don't believe you should assume anything unless a body turns up."

"Or part of one," Dorothy nodded.

Boom! The patio door rattled, and when Eugene opened it, there Eleanor stood panting something fierce. "Agnes Barton, don't you do that to me again. I was so worried!" She walked inside and stood next to Dorothy who had a smile plastered on her face.

"Not too much or you would have stayed with us," I scolded her. "Dorothy was a big help, though." I knew that would goad Eleanor, but she deserved it.

Her bottom lip trembled slightly. "I'm awful sorry. I promise it won't happen again."

Dorothy's eyes were still cast on Eugene as I made the introductions, leaving out the part that El and I were senior snoops. "We won't take up more of your time. Your room looks quite tidy so we'll be moving on."

"I'm a neat freak."

"Personally, I haven't met a freak yet that I didn't like," Eleanor said smiling sheepishly.

He grinned and gave Dorothy's hand another kiss before we shuffled out the door. Once we were in the hallway, Dorothy gushed. "What a wonderful man."

I frowned. "I wonder." I then informed Eleanor what Eugene had said.

"I hope you told that man you were married," Eleanor said to Dorothy.

"Of course I did. What kind of woman do you take me for?"

"Do you really want an answer?" El hinted. When Dorothy fell silent, El added, "Just as I thought."

"What are you worried about, Eleanor? You have been flirting with my Frank for years. I'm betting you would love a chance to put your claws into him."

"First off, I'm not worried about anything, and second, I don't need a man. I have Mr. Wilson."

Dorothy rolled her eyes at that. "Mr. Wilson looks ready to kick the bucket any day now."

"He's looked like that for years, dear," El said. "And he's stronger than he looks."

I nodded. "Yes, you should see him stroll out of Eleanor's house. He has a spring in his step that didn't get there via physical therapy."

"Yup," El added. "He really works out, if you get my drift."

Chapter Six

Dorothy stomped down the hall a few feet with arms flung up. "Oh, Eleanor! You just ruined it. Didn't you see that man was quite taken with me?"

"That should make you wonder why," Eleanor said.

I stepped between the two of them. "Yes, why you and not either of us?"

Dorothy smiled slyly. "He obviously has taste."

"He was ogling you for sure. If Frank—"

"Don't you dare tell him, Agnes Barton, or else ... I'll do something just awful to you."

El got in Dorothy's face. "Besides be in our company?"

Dorothy strode away. "I'm going to find my husband."

El and I stared at each other. "Well, I never," El said. "Something has to be wrong here. What gives?"

"I'm not sure, but I think we better keep an eye on Dorothy so she doesn't get herself into any trouble."

We followed in Dorothy's wake. We had worked hard enough, in my opinion, and I was hungry and we still had no room to speak of. I was beat and I'm sure El felt the same way as she was whistling as she breathed. Poor dear was all tuckered out.

When we walked into the dining room, we encountered Bridgett. "All done already, ladies?"

"We're not spring chickens, you know. I'd like

something to eat and be shown to our rooms."

"When you finish, I'll be happy to take you there."

"Maybe I didn't make myself clear. I mean now, before Eleanor falls out right here. That won't look too good on your brochure."

Bridgett pressed her lips into a line. "Fine," she snapped. "Come along."

We followed her down the hall and she opened a room with two beds and a solitary window. I frowned when I saw the beds weren't even made. "I thought you knew we were coming."

"I did, but be a dear and make your own beds. I have to get back to work."

"Yes, go back and watch everyone work. It seems that's what you do best," El spat.

Bridgett's features darkened. "You have no idea how hard it is to keep this place staffed properly. It took me all month to get the place full of residents."

"Might have something to do with the swamp out back," I pointed out. "Be a dear and have someone bring our luggage here."

"It's in the parlor. I'm sure you won't mind getting it yourself. After all, you are the hired help."

El put a finger in the air. "Are we being paid?"

"No, you're given room and board. You have no idea how expensive it is in Florida to live for the winter." She frowned. "I was under the impression that you two couldn't afford to stay elsewhere."

"And who told you that, dear?" I asked.

"Well, the sheriff back in Michigan." Bridgett whirled around and left before either of us could say another word.

I opened the small closet and found bedding and put it on the beds while Eleanor watched from a chair. I didn't mind that she just watched. Eleanor had puffy, dark circles under her eyes and I knew she was tired.

Eleanor got up. "At least we have a window with a view."

I moved to her side, glanced out and grimaced. There was a huge green dumpster directly out the window. "I'm beginning to wonder if we should just head back to Michigan."

"We can't, Aggie. We have to find out why those women turned up missing and what happened to them. Somebody here knows the truth. We just have to find out who."

I batted at my tears. "I know you're right. That Bridgett is just so awful, though."

"And Eugene was ogling Dorothy's jewels."

"Her what?"

"Jewelry, dear."

"Oh, I noticed that too, Eleanor. He seemed to be steering us toward the alligator theory, too."

"That's odd," she yawned. "Why would you presume anything when it comes to a missing person?"

"Unless it's to throw us off the trail."

Eleanor lay down on the bed and was asleep within minutes. I went to the parlor and nodded at a gentleman who stood at the door. I ran and hugged him tightly. "Oh, Andrew. I had so hoped you would show." I pulled away, admiring his slicked back grey hair and the white Bermuda shorts hugging his lean hips. He hooked his sunglasses on his white tee and smiled back.

"I had hoped to make the flight, but I knew that

wasn't going to happen. I'm glad to see you here at last."

"Apparently, we're the hired help," I informed him. "Eleanor is sleeping in the miniscule room they gave us. It has a view of the dumpster," I whined.

"Don't worry, dear. I'll see what I can do about that."

"Just the rooms. I think it might be a good idea if we kept the jobs for now." I moved in closer. "Two maids have disappeared," I whispered.

"Before you came or after?" he grinned.

"Before, silly. I never have worked so hard. Maids are underpaid and overworked."

Andrew went off in search of Bridgett and I went back to listening to Eleanor snore. Two maids missing. What an odd turn of events. Did Sheriff Peterson deliberately want us to investigate this case? And what about the packet of cash I had stashed in the locker? Who did it really belong to? All good questions that needed an answer. I just hoped that between us, we could figure out what was going on before one of us went missing ourselves.

Chapter Seven

An hour later El and I had settled in a spacious room on the first floor with a patio that faced the swamp, but at least we could view plenty of wildlife from that vantage point. I was even surprised to see a crane swooping low, a bird I thought was in reduced numbers in Florida. I could do without the spiders that were lying in wait on intricate webs near the top of the sliding door. For all I knew, the brown spiders might be a widow of some sort. I heard that there were three of the poisonous varieties here in Florida.

I wandered back inside and lounged on the white velour sofa. There was also a matching loveseat and glass-topped coffee table with a vase filled with pink roses. I wondered if Andrew supplied the flowers. In the bedroom, there were two queen-sized beds covered with pink and yellow quilts and a decent sized closet.

There was a rap at the door and I answered it to a beaming Andrew, who held a bottle of white zinfandel cradled in his arms. I opened the door more and he moved inside, finding crystal wine glasses without any prompting from me.

"Hey, have you been here before?" I asked.

"What makes you think that?" he smirked.

"Our hasty relocation to a beautiful room."

He poured the wine and handed me a glass. "I simply suggested that you were all leaving if you weren't given a larger room."

"Are you dodging my question?"

"Come now, Aggie. When have I ever withheld information from you before?"

"Like on every case."

He laughed at that. "So you plan to look into the disappearance of the maids I take it."

"Of course. Why would you think otherwise?"

"Why can't you just enjoy your time in Florida?"

"I'm not enjoying being a maid, but I wasn't given the choice, remember? It's not going to hurt us to do a little investigating while we are here."

He frowned. "Is that always the way it's going to be? Are you that consumed with putting yourself in danger?"

"Andrew! I thought you knew who I was by now."

"I do, but that doesn't mean I have to like it. On your last case, both El and you were nearly killed. When is it going to be enough for you?"

I didn't know what to say. *Why is he being like this?* "I didn't mean for that to happen, but please don't ask me to quit because I can't. I am a born snoop. You certainly didn't mind when I was working for you back in Saginaw, Michigan."

"You were an investigator, sure, but you were never put into dangerous situations. I never had to worry, but now—"

"Stop, please. Can't we enjoy tonight without fighting?"

He took a sip of his wine, and although his face was riddled with frown lines, he attempted a smile. "I guess. It's like I'm talking to a wall. You're never going to change and all I can do is decide if I can deal with it."

I was taken aback, but sipped my wine until Eleanor appeared with a beaming Mr. Wilson. "Great, it's couples night," El said. Her face then fell. "Who died?"

"Nobody, yet!" Andrew spat. "All I wanted was a peaceful night, but I guess my temper got the best of me." He downed his wine, strode toward the door and left with a slam of the door.

"Oh, my," El exclaimed.

"Oh, my, indeed," I retorted. "He's mad because I'm dead set on investigating the maids' disappearances."

Mr. Wilson shuffled toward the door. "I better calm the old boy down," he said as he left.

"So much for him saying he loves me not long ago. He doesn't like who I am."

"Just because a man loves you doesn't mean he has to love everything about you, just the most important parts," she said with a wink. "Of course, we could always investigate the recent robbery at the jewelry store in town."

"What do you mean recent? The same one the girl in town told us about?"

She shook her head. "Nope. Apparently it happened a half-hour ago."

My eyes widened. "Well, we better get into town before the dust settles."

El's shoulders dropped. "And how are you planning to do that when we have no transportation?"

"Leave it to me. I'm sure someone will loan us a ride."

I left the wine where it was and followed El out the

door. As we made it downstairs I spotted Darcy White, the cook, noted by her all-white uniform. "Hey, Darcy."

She turned her dark head in our direction. "Hello, you must be Agnes and Eleanor. The kitchen is closed until tomorrow."

"Yes, but I was wondering if you could give us a lift into town?"

She rubbed her large belly encased underneath her uniform. "Sure, but you'll have to find your own way back."

"Great," I said. "I'm sure we could find a way home."

We piled into Darcy's Impala and soon were tooling toward the boardwalk area of Turtle Dune Beach. We exited the car and waved to Darcy as she whipped from the curb. I inhaled deeply of the fragrances of bratwursts being cooked on storefront grills. El's eyes widened at the sight of bikini-clad beachgoers. Let's just say they show a little more skin here in Florida than they do in Michigan. I thought to ask for directions to the jewelry store, but police cruisers were parked in front of a place called Julie's Jewels, announced by the bold gold letters atop a large wooded sign.

We bought brats and munched on them until Sheriff Calvin Peterson approached us.

"Why are you two in town? I thought Bridgett was planning to keep you busy at the retirement village."

I looked behind him. "What's going on? I heard there was a robbery at the jewelry store."

His face reddened. "I hope that's not why you're here in town because as I told you earlier, there will be no snooping on my watch."

"Then don't watch and you won't see us."

El blinked her eyes. "Yeah, Sheriff."

He threw up his arms. "This isn't Michigan. I won't stand for this. It's dangerous here in Turtle Dune Beach. I'd hate to have two old ladies getting offed. What would my brother Clem say?"

He'd be happy, I thought. But who knows? Maybe Calvin is a man of a different cloth, but so far it's the same old thing. "I'm not sure, but he has always allowed us to investigate in the past."

"More like tolerated it. It's no wonder he sent you two old birds south for the winter."

Eleanor shook a fist at the sheriff. "Who you calling old?"

The sheriff wiped his large nose with a tissue and then replied, "The both of you."

"Calvin Peterson," a woman bellowed. "That's no way to talk to a senior citizen." She turned toward us, her silver hair sparkling of glitter. "I taught him better than that and I'm sorry if my boy has offended you ladies. He's just caught up with the recent robberies and is just so touchy."

The good sheriff pulled at his collar. "I meant no disrespect, ladies," he apologized. He turned toward the woman with the glitter hair. "I'm sorry, Mom, but geez ... these ladies are senior snoops and trying to interfere with the investigation."

I smiled at Peterson's mom. "I'm Agnes Barton and I didn't even get a chance to ask any questions, yet."

Eleanor waved. "I'm Eleanor Mason. And your name is?"

She rubbed an invisible wrinkle from her blue dress.

"Edith Stone. I remarried after Hal and I divorced."

"You were married to Hal Peterson? Sorry, but I just can't picture that," I said respectfully.

"Was he that randy back in the day?" Eleanor asked.

She laughed. "Why yes, he was. One of the reasons I had Clem and Calvin so close together. I couldn't keep him off me."

"He was a sheriff too, right?"

Calvin's eyes bulged. "Mother, do you really want to divulge family business to a couple of senior snoops?"

"Get back to work, Calvin. I can handle my own business."

Calvin sauntered away, but I could tell he didn't want to leave. I personally would love to learn more about the Peterson clan.

"Getting back to your question, yes, Hal was once an Iosco County sheriff until after the Robinson murders. Folks kinda turned against him when a suspect was never arrested."

"How sad. It's not like it was his fault. Besides the handyman, who else did they have to suspect?"

"We solved that cold case," El informed her.

"I heard that. It's a good thing you ladies are in town, what with missing maids at a retirement village in town and now two jewelry store robberies."

"Two?"

"I told you as much, Aggie," Eleanor reminded me.

I watched as the squad cars left the scene. "I'd sure love to question the clerk of the jewelry store."

"I'd be happy to introduce you to Julie. She's the

owner. I bet the poor dear is beside herself now."

We followed Edith inside and she introduced us to Julie Jacob, the owner. Julie stood shaking as she rifled through a stack of paperwork.

"I'm sorry about your troubles," I said. "I'm an experienced private investigator and would be happy to help if I could."

She tucked her hair behind her ears. "Help how?"

"Well, finding the person responsible."

Her brown eyes met mine. "That's what the police do, isn't it?"

El puffed up her chest. "Yes, when they are not—"

I cut El off. "Busy. What with budget cuts and what not it's a wonder any crimes are ever solved. At least, that's how it is in Michigan."

"Yeah," El started. "Cut protection and give pay bonuses to the city leaders."

"If you could answer a few questions we'll be out of your hair."

"Sure. Anything to delay me calling this in to my insurance company. My rates will be going up for sure as this is the second robbery in my store. I might even have to close up shop," she said tearfully.

I handed her a tissue from a box that sat on the counter. "What did the suspect look like?"

"He was tall and thin."

"How about his facial features?

"He wore a black ski mask and all dark clothing."

"Any cameras here in the store?"

"The police took them, but truthfully they were outdated. I had planned to upgrade them, but—"

"You were robbed again."

"Yes. After you leave, I'm locking up until I have them in place."

"Smart move. Were there any other customers in here at the time?"

"No, just the man with the gun."

"He held you by gunpoint?" El asked. "How awful."

She sniffled. "Yes."

"You need a gun in the store," El pointed out. "Back in Michigan, I always have mine at the ready."

"But of course you didn't bring it with you, right?" I asked El.

"Gosh no, then those guys at Homeland Security would have strip searched us."

"They did Martha."

"Whatever happened to her by the way?" El asked. "I haven't seen her since we jumped off the bus earlier."

"Who knows with my daughter," I said. "She'll show up. I'm sure of it."

"I'm sorry I can't give you any more info, but it's hard with a man wearing a ski mask."

"We'll canvas the neighborhood. Somebody had to have seen the perp leaving."

"Oh, I almost forgot. He left via the back door."

"Lead the way, dear."

Julie locked the front door and showed us out into an alley. I shook my head. One end surfaced on the beach and the other on the main drag. He could have easily slipped into the crowd unnoticed. We waved at Julie and we made our way up and down the alley looking for clues. "No discarded ski mask."

"Or bags," El chimed.

Just then, a man surfaced on the end of the alley and stood staring at us. When we made way for him, he sprinted away. We rounded onto the main drag and were in front of a newspaper stand when shots rang out.

I yelled, "Duck!"

Bullets peppered the news stand and bits of paper were flung into the air, raining down on us like snowflakes. El and I of course were huddled on the ground and had managed to crawl behind a parked Cadillac Seville.

"Holy cow!" Eleanor gasped. "We just got here and someone tried to off us."

"That can't be good."

El's eyes practically were bugged out. "Nope."

"They couldn't have been aiming for us. We haven't been here long enough to piss somebody off already."

"Well, the sheriff wasn't too happy we were planning to investigate."

"I think it's safe to say it wasn't the sheriff, El."

"It might be the man in the alley. He might be the jewelry thief."

Sirens blasted the air and soon we were surrounded with bubble lights via ten squad cars. None other than Sheriff Peterson helped us to our feet. "Are you ladies okay?" he asked, concern mirrored in his eyes.

"Yes, I think so," I replied.

"You weren't just whistling Dixie when you told us this town was dangerous," El said. "Does this happen regularly?"

"No, but there certainly has been an increase in

crime. I'm just glad you weren't hurt. I'd hate to hear what my brother would say if you were."

"You certainly have changed your tune."

"Just because I was upset you were going to investigate doesn't mean I want something untoward to happen to you." He wiped his brow with a hanky. "And my mother seems fond of you, too. Otherwise she'd never have spoken up to me like that. I assure you, I don't make a habit of making fun of older folks. If I did, I'd be run out of town on a rail. Florida depends on you northern folks flocking here every winter."

I felt bad for thinking ill of the sheriff.

"Did you see a gunman?" he asked us.

I shook my head. "No, but we spotted a man in the alley that sure tore off when he saw us moving toward him."

He pulled out a pad of paper. "Did you get a good look at him?"

"Not really. How about you, El?"

She shuddered. "He was tall and thin like the lady at the jewelry store said her robber was, but who knows if it was the same man."

"Seems to me the robber would be long gone," I said.

"I'd agree with you on that one, Agnes. No way would he be back."

El put a finger in the air. "Unless he left something behind in the alley. Maybe he was going back to get it before he was found out."

"Good point, El." I made a beeline for the alley with the sheriff in tow. He lent us his flashlight so we could see as it was beginning to get dark. I shined it along the wall and frowned when I spotted nothing out of the ordinary. I then motioned to the dumpster. “Might be a good place to check.”

Peterson took the flashlight and nodded to a nearby deputy who hopped in and came back up with a bag. Butterflies jumped in my belly as it was opened and jewels were pulled out.

“Of course!” I yelled. “He stashed the jewels with the hopes of coming back later to retrieve them,” I pointed out. “I bet that way nobody on the street would think anything was amiss. Did anyone report seeing someone suspicious after the robbery?”

“Not as of yet, but we are forming a task force. We need to find this perp before he strikes again.”

“At least Julie has her jewels back. It must have been just awful being robbed twice by the same man.”

“True,” the sheriff said. “Come back out here so we can talk more. I’m sure impressed about you finding those jewels.”

“Well, your deputy did most of the work. I just made an educated guess.”

“Lucky for you we were in the alley,” El said. “I do wonder if it was the same guy who shot at us.”

“That seems logical now, El, but he kinda did himself in. We might never have found the goods. All he would have had to do was wait.”

“Maybe he knows we senior snoops are too good to miss a clue like that, Aggie.”

“I guess, but to resort to murder in the same day? That’s just scary. I hope you catch this man sheriff, before he strikes again.”

“Can we catch a ride back to the retirement village?" El asked trembling. "I have had enough excitement for one day."

The sheriff nodded. "I can't blame you. I'll have my deputy take you back so I can finish up here."

We sat in the back seat and it was quite the sight. There were throngs of onlookers gawking at the scene, spent cartridges, deputies questioning witnesses. Not even the tantalizing fragrances from the candy shops could bring me out of the mood I was in.

El and I were nearly killed tonight and that didn't settle well with me. It's like everything Andrew had worried about came to pass. I had once again put myself and El and into harm's way.

Chapter Eight

The deputy dropped us off at the door of the retirement village and Bridgett and Andrew awaited us when we strode through the door. My eyes widened when he hugged me tight and as he pulled away, he asked, "Are you okay?"

"The sheriff called and told me what happened," Bridgett said. "I wish you'd tell me before you gallivant into town."

"I didn't think it would be that huge of a deal."

"Not until the bullets began to fly," El added. "I'm going to get a pistol tomorrow."

"Not if you're staying here, you're not," Bridgett gasped. "What would the residents think?"

"That we just don't clean their rooms, but are here to protect them."

"Bridgette is right, El. It's not safe. I mean, what if someone used it against you?"

"They'd have to pry it from my dead fingers first."

I gasped. "That almost happened today, El. Don't say things like that."

"I'm with Aggie on that one. I'd be lost without either of you." Andrew turned toward me. "I'm sorry I left earlier. I love who you are even if it's dangerous, but please be careful."

"We found the jewelry store's missing jewels," El told him. She then told him how it happened.

"Well, you girls sure have been busy, but I think we should turn in before it gets any later," he winked.

"Not here, you're not, Mr. Hart. I run an up and up business here. All residents are married," Bridgett said.

I frowned. "What is this, the 50's?"

El snickered as she whispered, "What she doesn't know won't hurt her."

For the time being, I'd play along. "We need to finish that bottle of wine. Goodnight, Bridgett."

She glared at us as we made for our room. Once we rounded a corner, Andrew pulled me in for a good smooching until an arguing Frank and Dorothy Alton strode up.

"Oh, Frank. That Eugene Bragsworth is a decent man. I swear that I'd never cheat on you."

"Is that why you never took your eyes off him all evening?"

She wrung her hands. "I'm sorry. I didn't mean to. I swear."

We moved past the pair as none of us wanted to get involved. Once we were in our room, Andrew asked, "Who is Eugene Bragsworth?"

"He's a man we met earlier. He seems taken with Dorothy."

"Crazy man is what he is," El spat. "If Dorothy doesn't watch it, she'll lose Frank."

"That should make you happy. Since when have you and Dorothy gotten along?"

"I have been trying is all I can say, Aggie. I'm just worried about them. It's so unlike Frank to get mad at Dorothy like that."

Andrew sat down and poured us both a glass of

wine and we tipped it back. Yuck, it was warm now. Not that it was my fault, but I should have chilled it after Andrew ran off. I smiled to myself. I'm so glad that Andrew had a change of heart. I'd hate to say where we'd be if he hadn't. One thing was for certain, though. I had no plans to change.

Andrew's eyes glowed from the light of the candle that Eleanor hastily lit before dodging out in search of Mr. Wilson. "So what gives, Aggie?"

"Who, me?" I laughed. "Besides enjoying a quiet moment with the man I love, nothing."

"Why do I smell smoke then?"

I sipped my wine. "Maybe because you want to smell it."

"I'm serious, Aggie. Be careful."

"I am. I hadn't expected to run into the trouble El and I did. All I wanted to do was question the woman who owns Julie's Jewels. Honest."

"Julie's Jewels? That's funny."

I wrung my hands. "The poor owner has been robbed twice within days. I felt bad for her, but at least some of the jewels were recovered."

"True, but I thought you were looking into the disappearance of the missing maids?"

"I was, but how could I pass up a jewelry store robbery?"

"You say it like you did it."

"No, I don't have a criminal bone in my body and I'm a horrible liar."

He rubbed my cheek affectionately. "I think you're pretty good at avoiding the truth, if you ask me."

"Don't tease. You know you love it."

"Let's take this conversation into the bedroom."

"Oh, Andrew, you take my breath away."

And like two love-sick people half our age, we reacquainted ourselves in the room meant for love. I just hoped Eleanor stayed away long enough for us to seal the deal.

***

Early the next morning, Eleanor thumped around in the other room loud enough for me to hear her, and I joined her in the living room. "You don't have to make so much racket. Andrew's gone."

"What do you mean gone?" she chuckled. "Like deceased?"

"Oh, please. He has some old friends in Tampa he wanted to drop by and see."

"Well, I guess that leaves us all alone to do what we do best." She rubbed her hands together. "Dig for clues."

I nodded. "How was Mr. Wilson this morning?"

"Very much alive. He loves his job in the kitchen and his tuna casserole is on the menu for lunch."

"At least someone loves their job. I could stand an easier one. I guess I better get shower bound so we can get started. I'd hate to make Bridgett mad."

"Since when do you care for her? You said—"

"We can't very well question the woman if she is at odds with us and after last night. I think she might at least be keeping closer tabs on us."

"That's not good. How are we going to investigate with her breathing down our necks?"

"We're going to play it cool until we at least question her. She might offer us some insight into why the maids went missing."

I took my shower turning the gold faucets on. Obviously, whoever built this retirement village had spent their money well, because it was beautiful. I was thankful for the glass shower doors. There would be no Psycho moments for me. I loved to be able to see who was coming at me at any given moment.

My thoughts trailed off to Duchess, my cat. I sure missed her and hoped Trooper Sales was treating her well. I'd have left her with my granddaughter, Sophia, but the poor dear had been so sick as of late.

When I had toweled off I slipped into an orange capri and tee set, tugging on canvas shoes since I was planning to clean for most of the day. To heck with wearing that unflattering uniform. As I strolled out, it was to the sight of Eleanor in her bra and grannies trying with all her might to squeeze into a purple tee and denim capris. Two long breaths and gasps later, she was dressed and raised a brow. "What are you gawking at, Aggie? I'm not the only one who has packed on a few."

I patted my mid section. "Don't remind me, old girl. I know I have let myself go. It must be all that good lovin' I'm getting."

"All the good lovin' we're both getting," she said with a smirk. "I need some more clothes. Maybe we should do some shopping later, or better yet, head off to the beach. I have never been to the ocean."

"I promise we'll do both today, but let's get a move on before we have to spend the entire day cleaning rooms."

With that, we both left the room and found our housekeeping carts. I emptied the vacuum bags with a shake and found myself covered in dust. Eleanor laughed at me until I threw a dust bunny on her. Eleanor's face was all dust except for her eyes and I cackled at her.

Her hands flew to her hips. "What you laughing at, dusty?" She proceeded to rub her finger across my face and came back with her finger layered in grime.

"That's a good one, El."

Just then, Dorothy walked up on us. "Wh-What happened girls?"

"Great, Dorothy, get your cart."

"I can't. Eugene is taking me sightseeing today."

"What about Frank?" El gasped.

"He's being a fuddy duddy. Plus, he won't even know I'm gone. He's working in the kitchen."

I couldn't believe her. "That doesn't make it right, Dorothy. How would you feel if Frank was cavorting with another woman?"

"Humph. Don't be a sour puss just because your man left. I deserve a little fun."

Dorothy trounced off, leaving El and me with our mouths agape. Until the coughing started that is. All I could taste was dust! I shoved the carts into our room. That way, Bridgett would think we were working. El and I then cleaned ourselves up a tad and set off downstairs. I slipped into the kitchen and came back with Darcy's keys to her Impala dangling from my fingertips. Soon we zoomed out of the parking lot and made our way toward town.

"How are we supposed to find Dorothy and Eugene?" El asked. "There could be a million places they could hole up."

"Like where?"

"If we can't figure out where they would they go sightseeing. We're never going to find them."

"Stop being so negative. We have to find them before Dorothy does something she'll regret."

Truth was, I had no clue how to find them, but that was before I saw them walking arm in arm on the boardwalk, ducking into a seafood restaurant. I hurried and parked, ambling toward the restaurant called Clammy's. I hushed Eleanor as she began to laugh. "We need to be on the down low."

We sat a few tables over from Dorothy, and El and I were buried behind the neon blue menus. We sat next to a tank full of lobsters. Strange, I had thought this was a crab shack with a name like Clammy's. Either that, or someone was hot and sticky here.

"I wonder what's the deal with Eugene Bragsworth?" I whispered to El.

"Beats me, but he's holding her hand."

My eyes widened. "How could she?"

Eleanor shrugged. "Maybe he's some kind of Don Juan."

"Mr. Bragsworth is itching to have a smack down." I pursed my lips. "This really steams my kettle. Dorothy and Frank have been married for over fifty years."

"I know. If anything, I expected Frank to be the one roaming. Dorothy is such a shrew," El spat. "What is wrong with her?"

We clammed up when Dorothy's giggles could be heard. "Oh, Bragsworth, you're too funny. I'm not beautiful. I'm an old woman."

One with a husband, I thought. My eyes widened when Eugene kissed the back of Dorothy's hand. Obviously, Dorothy had taken leave of her senses, and we'd better intercede before it gets more out of hand.

I stood and ran straight into a waiter carrying a silver tray. His eyes bulged as steamed crabs and lobsters thumped to the floor and everyone's eyes bored into me. "What?" I said. "I didn't mean to hit you, young man."

From between gritted teeth he stated, "That's okay, ma'am, but that's a hundred dollars worth of seafood on the floor."

"She said she was sorry," Eleanor blurted out. "I hope you're not suggesting she pay for it. I mean, us senior citizens are on a fixed income."

"Of course not, I just—"

"Wanted to make her feel worse than she already does. It's bad enough she has made a spectacle of herself."

"Thanks, El, I think." I brushed the melted butter from my shirt the best I could, but knew it was ruined. No way would I ever get the butter stain out now. I was given a club soda and I went into the restroom to try, at least, but it didn't help much. El stood at the ready and pressed the button on the automatic hand dryer where I tried to dry my shirt.

"Oh, it's hopeless," I whined.

"I told you we should go shopping."

"I suppose you're right. Hey, where did Dorothy and Bragsworth go? Are they still in the restaurant?"

"Nope, they left just as you tipped the tray over.

From the looks of the people out there, you'd think they'd never seen lobsters and crabs fly," she chuckled. "Such a waste, but then again we weren't here for the food. Do you think Dorothy is planning to cheat on Frank?"

"I sure hope not. She's eighty, so maybe that's not in her thoughts."

"So am I, dear. And it's always in my thoughts," El said with a wink.

"True, but I have high hopes that you'll change your wicked ways."

"I will when you do."

"Let's just go shopping. I doubt we'll find Dorothy again, which worries me. She's not used to a handsome man whispering sweet nothings in her ear."

"Maybe he's just interested in her jewels. He sure was eyeing them up the other day."

"I know. If he was younger I'd have thought he might be our jewel thief."

"Well, he is tall and thin, but I doubt he has the ability of bounding away so quick and shooting at us."

"I have to agree with you, Eleanor. He doesn't look like the type who would try and kill someone."

"Then of course, you just never know. We should find out if he was in town yesterday afternoon. That was when the robbery happened."

"I think we're overdue with questioning Bridgett, too. I hope she has something to share once she gets over being mad because we didn't clean yet today.

Chapter Nine

El and I made our way into a boutique called Nina's. Bright pink apparel hung on the walls and there was a register toward the front with sparkly jewelry displayed in a locked glass case. We rummaged through the racks, moving vibrantly colored apparel with a sweep of our fingertips until we found our sizes. We then wandered toward the dressing rooms.

"What is that smell?" a woman asked.

"It smells just like fish," another volunteered. "I hate fish."

"Then why do you live by the ocean, Glenda?" the first woman asked.

"You know why, Nancy. I love all the diverse nightlife here."

El walked toward the woman. "Excuse me, ladies. Did I hear you say something about nightlife?"

"Why, yes," Nancy said. "We have an all-male show this evening."

El's eyes bulged. "Do you mean strippers?"

"Yes," she giggled, tucking her grey hair behind her ears. "It's not just for the younger folks, you know."

"Oh, I know," El replied. "Believe me, I'm eighty. That's the new twenty."

Glenda laughed. Her silver hair sparkled like spray-on glitter was applied. "It's at Ramón's on the beach. The doors open at seven and the show starts at nine."

She pressed a card into El's hand. "Hand this to the man at the door and he'll show you to our table. We'll both be there."

"Thanks. I'm Eleanor Mason and this is my partner in crime, Agnes Barton. We're senior snoops."

"Aren't we all, dear," Nancy said with a wink. "I wish I knew where that smell was coming from."

"It's me, I'm afraid," I told the ladies. "I had a run in with a tray of lobster and crab. I believe the juice got all over me. That's why we're here. I need some new clothes fast."

"Oh, what a horrible accident. I ran into a dessert tray just last week and looked like a cream puff afterward," Glenda said. "And I don't even like cream puffs."

"See you tonight," Nancy said. "We gotta run now."

El and I went into the dressing room and I put on pink pants with a matching shirt that had a flamingo embroidered on it. When I surfaced, El was dressed in a bright yellow pants suit. "Wow," I exclaimed. "You look great. You clean up real good."

She rubbed her hands together. "I can't wait for the stripper show tonight. It's about time I get to see some buff skin for a change."

"Hey, how about Mr. Wilson?"

"I said buff, Aggie, not saggy," she laughed. "What Mr. Wilson doesn't know won't hurt him."

"True. It hasn't bothered him that he has forgotten his first name so I guess this won't bother him. Lucky for me my Andrew is out of town. I'd hate to have to explain to him about why we're going."

"Well, we girls need to have fun, too."

The front door to the shop slammed closed and we stood face-to-face with a gunman. The same one from the alley, but this time he wore a ski mask. “Hands up, grandmas,” he hissed.

We trembled as we put up our hands. Not straight up, but up enough for the man to know we were complying. The woman behind the counter began to cry. “Please don’t hurt anyone. Just take what you want.”

“I want those jewels in the case, and be speedy about it.”

She opened the case with trembling hands and shoved the jewels into a brown paper bag that the gunman supplied, and hastily handed over the goods. “Please, that’s all I have.”

“Now hand over your rings, ladies.”

I gasped. No way was I handing this man over my mother’s ring. “Just go. I’m not giving you my jewels.”

He walked toward me and put the gun to my head, but before he had time to do more Eleanor gave him a kick. He hobbled and howled until he heard sirens and he ran out the door, disappearing into the throng of people outside.

I let out a sigh. “Forget what I said before. We need to get a gun, Eleanor.”

“Aggie, that man almost killed you. When a gunman says give him your jewels, just do it next time.”

We waited until the sheriff appeared and then began to spout off what happened.

“Aggies was almost killed by that perp. What kind of town are you running here and how does he keep getting away so quick?” Eleanor asked.

“Did you recognize the man?”

"No. He did look like the same man we saw yesterday by the alley, but he wore a mask." I turned toward the clerk, a skinny blond. "Do you have any cameras?"

"Yes." She ran into the back and handed the disc recording to the sheriff. "I was s-so scared. I wish I had never started carrying real gems here. This was the last thing I had expected. It's no wonder Julie's Jewels closed."

"Not for good, I hope," I said. "You can't let this madman ruin your security. Sure it's scary, but you have to go on like business as usual."

"You could always hire an armed security officer," El suggested.

"Or have your own gun for your protection."

The woman quivered. "I-I don't like that idea. I'm afraid of guns."

"It was just a suggestion, dear. Of course you did the right thing. You should always hand over what a gunman asks for."

"Then why didn't you?" El asked.

"Because, silly, Martha just bought me this ring."

"I'm wondering if we'll ever see her again," El mused. "She's been gone a long time."

"This is Florida. I'm sure she's soaking up the rays somewhere with a cocktail and a male companion."

After a lengthy pause the sheriff chimed in. "I'm glad everyone is okay. I wish I knew how to stop this man before he strikes again."

"You need more cops on the streets."

"This is a tourist town and we are trying our best. We just don't have enough resources."

"I know you are. I didn't mean to sound like I was

blaming you. It's just so frustrating for me when I see an ongoing crime wave." I had my own ideas, like wondering if Bragsworth could be behind the robberies. He was tall and thin, too, but I didn't recognize his voice as the one of the robber unless he was masking it. And we had seen him with Dorothy not long ago.

"We'll be heading back to Sunny Brooke unless you have any more questions, Sheriff."

"No, but I'm sure we'll be in touch. Please use caution when you're out and about. Clem would be awful mad if I let something happen to the two of you."

I doubted that, but I nodded and we made our purchases and left in search of the Impala … if only I could remember where I had parked it. After we circled the block a few times, we found it and we piled into it in exhaustion. I drove back to Sunny Brooke and hoped to duck Bridgett, but it wasn't happening.

"Where were you ladies? The residents are complaining that their rooms haven't been cleaned yet."

"We were looking for Dorothy Alton," I informed her, which was the truth.

"She's upstairs working on the second floor."

Working what, I wondered. "Oh, okay. We'll start cleaning right away." Eleanor sighed noisily. "Come on, El."

We pushed our housekeeping carts out and began cleaning rooms until we ran across Dorothy, who we cornered in a room near Bragsworth's. "Where were you earlier?" I grilled her.

"I-I went into town."

"With who?"

"Eugene Bragsworth. He's such a nice man, don't

you think?"

"Not really. What kind of man tries to romance a married woman? What would Frank think about you gallivanting around with that man?

She wrung her hands. "Oh, I-I don't know. Let's just keep it between us."

"Where did you go?" Eleanor asked with a raised brow.

"I don't know. We went to a lot of places, Eleanor. You don't expect me to remember them all, do you?"

"Did you have your eye on Bragsworth the whole time?" I asked.

"Yes, except for when he used the restroom," she giggled. "I'm a married woman, after all."

"That's interesting because there was another robbery. What time did you lose sight of him?"

"Seriously, Agnes, I can't say. I have short term memory loss."

"Likely story," Eleanor spat. "Did you kiss him?"

"Of course not! I do have some scruples. I'm not like you girls."

"And what is that supposed to mean?" Eleanor huffed.

"Well, just that you girls are a little on the loose side."

I gasped. "We are not. Why do people always say that? The only man in my life is Andrew Hart and I'm true to him even though we aren't married."

Eleanor's face was red. "Yeah, and I'm exclusive with Mr. Wilson."

"How long do you expect that to last, dear? He's a might frail."

"He has more spring in his step than a slinky," Eleanor assured her.

Changing the subject before it got more out of hand, I stated, "Seriously, Dorothy. We think Eugene Bragsworth might be the jewel thief."

"That's ridiculous. I was with him the whole time in town."

"You were almost with him the whole time. He could have run off and done the robbery while you waited for him," Eleanor pointed out. "Men can be tricky when they want to be and he was ogling your jewels."

"He sure was," Dorothy smiled. "I can't say the last time Frank has ogled anything."

"I meant your jewelry, not your womanly jewels," Eleanor said. "Frank has been quite generous with you and has bought you enough jewelry to stock Tiffany's."

"I know. That's why I came back to clean. Frank gave me quite the look when I came in the door with Bragsworth. I'll have to smooth things over later for sure."

"So you'll quit hanging around Bragsworth, then?" I asked. "Because I need to remind you, what do we really know about the man? He could be a jewelry thief or worse."

"Worse? You girls sure have an imagination. What's worse than a jewelry thief?"

"A killer. This jewelry thief shot at us yesterday. Don't let a man's sweet nothings fool you. This man has motives that we might all be clueless about."

Dorothy put up her hand. "You girls really are a couple of drama queens. Have you ever thought that maybe the man just enjoys my company?"

"Nope. It never occurred to me," El said.

Dorothy trounced away in a huff. She was either ignoring our warnings or thought we had gone plain loco.

"Well, Dorothy sure is set on believing Bragsworth is on the up and up."

Eleanor pushed the cart and knocked on a door, and when nobody answered, she used her skeleton key to open the door. "He might be, but I'm not feeling it. No man in his right mind romances a married woman."

I followed Eleanor into the room. "Plus, he fits the profile of the jewelry thief, but I suppose we'll have to wait and see how it plays out."

"Or we could go rifling through his drawers," Eleanor suggested.

"Would that be like dresser drawers or his regular drawers, like pants?"

"Do I have a choice?"

I smiled, but barely. "Knowing you, I have no idea which would be worse, but great idea."

We cleaned the room we were in and then made our way to Bragsworth's room. After a brief knock, we opened the door and Bragsworth stood there with a perplexed look on his face. Gone was the hint of smile we usually saw him wearing. The lines of his face were creased near his mouth and his eyes flashed at the two of us.

"I'm sorry. We're here to clean your room if you don't mind."

He leaned against the doorframe. "Well, I do mind. It's not a good time for me."

I tried to look past him, but he gave me a sharp

look. "When would be? I'd really like to get done cleaning soon. That Bridgett gives us quite a tongue lashing when we don't get our work done."

"Actually, I'm not that untidy. I'll tell Bridgett that I won't be requiring your services. I can clean my own room," he informed us. With that he closed the door with a whoosh.

Eleanor's brows shot up. "Well, I'll be. He certainly wanted us out of there in a hurry."

"Maybe he's counting his jewels."

"He certainly looks guilty enough, but Aggie, we don't know he's guilty of the robberies yet. Maybe Dorothy let it slip that we're senior snoops. That would give him plenty of reason not to want us around."

"If he's guilty yes, but we haven't accused him of anything yet. We need more to go on than his body size matching the suspect."

"There could be plenty of other reasons for him not to want us around. Maybe he saw us at Clammy's. Maybe he's figured out that we are trying to talk Dorothy out of spending any more time with him."

"He couldn't know that unless Dorothy spilled the beans. We need to talk to her about keeping our suspicions just between us."

"You're talking about Dorothy here. We aren't on that good of terms with her yet, unless…."

"Unless what, dear?"

"We should involve her in our investigation. That way she'll be away from Bragsworth and more inclined to keep it zipped."

"Good idea, El. I knew we were friends for a reason."

We went in search of Dorothy once we had finished cleaning the rooms. I led the way as we went downstairs and met Dorothy in the dining room. The room had all round tables covered with white linen tablecloths. They had an area along one wall that was set up as a salad bar. Since all of the residents were able bodied, it wouldn't be a problem for them standing in line for any length of time. There was a double swinging door that led into the kitchen and I took it upon myself to enter, followed by Eleanor.

Fans roared overhead, but it didn't help much as the kitchen was stifling. We found Mr. Wilson cutting up onions with not one tear dotting his eyes.

"Hello, Wilson," I greeted him. "Don't those onions bother you?"

"Nope. I used to cut onions in the Navy."

"You worked in the kitchen then, too?"

"Yup. Hello, Peaches," he greeted Eleanor. "How's about us meeting in the bushes later tonight?"

"I-I can't. I'm working," she stalled.

Obviously she didn't want him to know about the all-male review we planned to see in the evening. "Yup. We're hot on the trail of a jewelry thief."

"That sounds dangerous. Be careful, Peaches," he told Eleanor. "I'd hate to have something happen to you. Who else would bother with me? I'm afraid folks think I'm too frail to be of much use."

Eleanor piped up. "That's ridiculous. You're more able bodied that any man I have ever known. You're strong as an ox and twice as—"

"Too much information," I cut in. "I get it."

"You don't have to be rude about it, Aggie."

"I wasn't trying to be. I was just stating a fact."

"That's something we need more of… *real facts* to catch this thief." She pursed her lips. "Have you heard any juicy gossip in the kitchen, Wilson?"

"Aside from the fact that Frank Alton is beside himself with worry about his wife hanging all over that fellow Eugene Bragsworth, no."

"He's that upset, huh?" I asked.

"Yes, and he's a military man. He's looking for a gun as we speak. I guess I shouldn't have told him there was a shotgun hanging in the game room."

We ran into the game room, which was the same area where both card and board games were played. It had a huge stone fireplace and I stared at the empty metal arms that I figured once held a shotgun. Who in their right mind would leave a gun out in the open like that? Hadn't Bridgett just told us we weren't allowed to have one?

We raced toward the elevator and caught Frank as he came out, the shotgun clasped in his capable hand and his eyes fixed with menacing intent.

"Stop, Frank!" I shouted.

He whirled. "Don't interfere here, Agnes. I'm going to teach that man not to try and trifle with my wife. I haven't put up with her nagging and bickering all these years to let some man just whisk her away now."

I tried to hide a smile that formed. "I know. I told Dorothy to stay clear of that man, but—"

"She wouldn't listen," Eleanor cut in. "But please give us some time."

"Eleanor's right. I plan to distract Dorothy long enough for her to come to her senses."

"Good luck with that one. I have been trying to do that for over fifty years now."

We were almost in front of Bragsworth's door when it flew open and Dorothy Alton strode out to Frank's side wringing her hands. "Oh, Frank! What are you doing with that gun? You're gonna get hurt."

"I'm going to kill that Casanova once and for all. Teach the man not to move in on my wife."

I gulped when Bragsworth surfaced at his door and held up his hands. "You got it all wrong. I'm not trying to sway your wife. We're just friends, I swear."

"I know all about your kind. You are sweet talking my Dorothy and she doesn't have sense enough to know you're up to no good."

"Are you calling me stupid, you old coot?" Dorothy bellowed.

"You aren't used to men like this and I'm putting an end to it." He pulled up the gun and Bragsworth ducked back into the room just as Frank popped off a shot. Wood splintered into the air and screams echoed down the hallway.

I couldn't find my voice for a minute as I was in shock. Where did the shotgun shells come from? As Frank pulled out a new shell, Eleanor yanked the shotgun from his hands. "Have you gone plain loco?" El shouted. "You could have killed the man."

"Yup, that'll teach him," he curtly nodded.

Soon seniors flew toward the sound of the shotgun blast followed by none other than Bridgett. "What on earth?" she asked. "What is the meaning of this?"

I crossed my arms. "I'd like to know that, too. Why is there a loaded shotgun hanging in the game room?"

"It wasn't loaded!" she shrieked.

I wasn't about to let her off this easily. "Then where did he find the shells?"

"How should I know?"

"They were in the drawer with the Monopoly game," Frank said.

I couldn't believe it! "What kind of games do you play here in Florida? We don't need shotgun shells to play Monopoly in Michigan."

"I thought you said no guns were allowed," Eleanor said in a whiny voice.

"Well, I didn't know there were shells in there. I guess I should have checked."

"I'm beginning to wonder about your qualifications. Obviously you're a woman of few details instead of being detail orientated."

"I assure you this was just an oversight. I promise both the shotgun and shells will be gone."

"Was it there when the maids disappeared?"

"Yes, but I'm sure it hasn't been used before."

"How can you be so sure?"

"The maids disappeared a few days after they started working here and the shotgun hasn't moved until now. I was there both nights when they disappeared, but I think they just ran off."

"Like chased?"

"No. I think they just quit. It's no secret that they felt underpaid and overworked."

"I can attest to that, but how do you know it wasn't a secret?"

"The maids had complained to Darcy, but before I could confront either of them, they were gone."

"Did you report them missing right away?"

"No, but when I did, the sheriff didn't believe they were truly missing either until we found their flip flops near the swamp."

"I see. Was a search party sent out into the swamp, at least?"

"Yes, but they never turned up anything. The police said they didn't expect to find anything. It's not like they could dive in the swamp looking for remains. It's dangerous in there."

"Well, then, why was one of them confirmed as dead?"

"The sheriff found Mary Lou's blood-stained clothing."

"Mary Lou?"

"Yes, Mary Lou Reacher. She was the first maid who disappeared, and then a few days later, Jenny Sue Smith disappeared. Both were never seen again."

"So we have two maids that just disappear into thin air and you think what?"

"That gators got them, of course. What else could I think?"

"That foul play was at hand. That there might be a more sinister reason they went missing."

"Yeah," Eleanor said. "How long has the jewelry thief been on the loose?"

"I don't see what this has to do with anything."

I leaned in. "So you're dodging the question?"

"No, I'm just not sure of the answer. You might want to take that up with the sheriff because I'm not sure."

"Really? Back home, small town gossip mills are a

great source of information."

"Gossip isn't that reliable."

"You'd be surprised. Plus, I'm not so sure if the sheriff would be so inclined to share with me the specifics of the robberies. But since you don't want to answer the question I suppose I should question the sheriff tomorrow. I hope you can overlook this little episode today."

She pointed at Frank. "You mean *that man* shooting up the place?"

I gazed at what remained of the doorframe. "How do you know who shot the door frame? You weren't even here."

"Bragsworth called the front desk."

"Was that before or after you heard the shotgun blast?"

"After, I guess."

"So you responded to a phone call before the sound of a shotgun going off?"

"I was right there! I couldn't ignore the call."

"Well, then, Frank was just overcome with emotion. Maybe Bragsworth should leave married women alone and he wouldn't have to worry about being nearly shot to death."

"That hardly excuses the man."

"True, but I'm sure it won't happen again. Right, Frank?"

"Nope. He can have my wife," he said as he stomped off.

"Oh, Frank," Dorothy called after him making tracks to keep up with him.

I stared at Bridgett in total silence until she finally

said, "Okay, I won't call in the sheriff this time, but you better get a handle on your friend Frank. He's a loose cannon!"

El and I watched Bridgett make way for the front desk and my blood was boiling. "Why do I feel like she's keeping something from us?"

El blinked her eyes. "Yeah. I think she knows more about the maids' disappearances than she is saying."

"And they are all going on with the alligator theory." I rubbed my brow as it was throbbing. My ears certainly were ringing after being so close when Frank unloaded the shotgun. "We are going to question the sheriff. Perhaps he will give us some information that would give us a reason to believe an alligator could be the culprit in the maids' disappearances. As it stands, I'm not buying it."

Chapter Ten

Eleanor sauntered from the bathroom wearing a blue, silken Chinese style dress with matching pants with white ballerina style flats on her feet. I laughed at the pink dragon design that trailed down the side of the dress.

"What are you laughing at?" She eyed my yellow blouse with matching slacks and white strap sandals. "Are you going to the stripper show dressed like that?"

"What's wrong with how I'm dressed?"

"You look like Jessica Fletcher in that getup." El pursed her lips. "That and you look way uptight."

I gasped. "Thanks, Eleanor. What a friend you are."

She picked at an invisible string on her dress. "I do my best," she giggled. "This is going to be so much fun."

I grinned, but barely. The truth was I had never been to a male stripper show. I sure hoped Andrew wouldn't hear about it. Dang Eleanor and her bright ideas, but no sense in stressing over it because no way was Eleanor letting me talk her out of going.

I poured a glass of wine and set it on the coffee table after taking a swig. My hands shook and my heart raced. "Are you sure you want to go?"

"You betcha. Plus, we're meeting some real Florida girls there. It's about time we mingle with the natives."

I had completely forgotten about Nancy and Glenda, who we had met at Nina's earlier in the day. I downed my wine and made way for the door. "Time to go. I hope you have your nitroglycerin with you, dear."

She tapped her white handbag that she had bought at Glenda's earlier in the day. "Right here in the bag." She frowned. "I do hope we can procure a handy sidearm. I miss my pistol."

"Bridgett said—"

"Oh, pooh. That from a woman who kept a shotgun and shells in the game room? That's something I'd expect from back home in Michigan."

We wandered downstairs where a taxi waited. Once we were settled into the back seat it took off toward town. We arrived five minutes later at Ramón's. It had a flashing neon sign that changed from pink to green. Two palm trees sat on either side of a red door with a doorman who was bare-chested and wore only a grass skirt and flip flops on his feet. Eleanor's eyes practically bugged out as she ogled the muscle-bound bald man with a tan that you could only get in Florida.

I handed the man at the door the card we were given earlier and he smiled. "Oh, you're a friend of Nancy and Glenda's."

We nodded. Even I couldn't keep my eyes off the doorman's muscle-bound frame. We were led to a table near the stage, which had a green vine centered on it and, of course, a stripper pole covered with green ivy. Raffia hung off the stage, nearly touching the floor. The interior of the club looked like a jungle with greenery hanging off each table. It had a Hawaiian feel to it with a pig roasting out on the patio from the way the fragrance wafted to us. All servers were dressed as hula girls with gourds for a bikini top and grass skirts around their trim waists. Eleanor looked to the tiki bar that was complete with bamboo framework and the bases of the barstools were carved with images of tiki gods.

I nodded at Nancy and Glenda, who were dressed in navy blue capris and white tees, dressed alike. We sat as Nancy motioned us to two chairs.

"Wow, they sure go all out here," I said.

Glenda gave her updo a careful pat. "They sure do. Just wait until you see the men."

"I haven't ever been to a male stripper show before," Eleanor said. "Do they go all the way?"

Nancy laughed. "No, but they sure wear some skimpy briefs. The kind that bares their buttocks."

Eleanor's eyes widened at that. "I can't wait, but I'm sure parched."

Glenda signaled a waitress who made her way toward us with a sway of her hips. "What can I get you ladies? Piña coladas are on special."

"We'll both have one," I said as I waved a twenty in the air.

She snatched up my money, whizzed away and returned with the drinks, each one with a pink umbrella inside. I took mine and sipped it, marveling at the smooth and tasty coconut pineapple blend. Within a second my eyes bulged and I pounded the table with my fist as I had a brain freeze.

"What's the matter, Aggie?" El asked.

I couldn't answer. My brain was too frozen.

"Are you having a stroke?" Nancy asked.

Glenda leaned forward. "Seizure?"

"No," I finally gasped. "Frozen headache."

"You should have seen your face contort," Eleanor laughed with tears rolling down her cheeks.

I glared at her. "I wouldn't laugh at you."

"Oh, yes you would."

I nodded in agreement. "Okay, you got me there."

Nancy chuckled. "It happens to the best of us."

"Yes, it sure does."

"Where are you ladies staying?" Glenda asked.

"At the Sunny Brooke Retirement Village."

Nancy bit down on her fist. "Oh, my, those poor maids."

"Mary Lou and Jenny Sue were so nice. And to think the alligators got them," Glenda added. "I was so sure that they'd close down that place after that."

Here we go again with the alligator theory. "Why is that?"

"Well," Glenda began. "It's an awful dangerous place to retire. If the hired help keeps getting knocked off then the residents are probably next."

"Or the new help," Nancy nodded in agreement. "I heard they hired some gals from the north to replace the girls."

I gulped. "They sure did. Us."

Glenda patted my hand. "So how is it there? Are the alligators roaming the property?"

"No, just out back in the swamp. It looks like they have a gate keeping them out now."

Eleanor shuddered, showering us with the scent of cheap perfume. "It's so scary here. First the maids disappeared and now a jewelry thief is running loose. Has there always been that much crime in Turtle Dune Beach?"

Nancy shook her head. "Oh, no. Please don't think badly of this town. We are a very tight knit community that welcomes our northern visitors with open arms."

"Do either of you think it odd that the owner of Sunny Brooke seems clueless about the disappearances?"

"Oh Bridgett, you mean. Well, she's a strange one. Word has it she'll do anything to keep the story out of the newspapers," Nancy informed us.

"Well, I saw a newspaper story about it," I insisted.

"Perhaps, but her brother owns the only paper in town and the story about the missing maids was only featured once," Nancy continued.

"Maybe it has something to do with the jewelry thief," I added.

Nancy's brow arched. "The maids' disappearances and the jewelry thief are connected?"

"It's too early to tell, but in my experience of an investigator, you just never know. Many cases are connected."

"What Aggie means is that the jewelry store robberies are bigger news right now," El clarified.

What I wondered about was why Bridgett would want to keep the maids' disappearances quiet? Was she afraid of it hurting her business or another, more sinister reason?

Just then, music started playing a club mix and a man who wore only a thong danced his way toward the stripper pole. He shimmied it, swinging from the vine and nearly touching the women at the tables near us. My eyes widened when a woman with wild, flowing hair and a jungle print cat suit, stood at the end of the stage waving a handful of ones in the air.

I blinked my eyes. It couldn't be, but it was my daughter Martha who had gone AWOL. I moved into action, but El stilled my movement. So I was resigned to watch my daughter shove a one dollar bill down the G-string of the stripper.

"Leave her be, Aggie," El shouted over the loud music. "She's just having fun."

"I want to know where in the hell she's been."

"She's young. Probably hanging out at the beach like I wished we could."

The man gyrated near Martha and pulled her on the stage. Suddenly a chair appeared and Martha sat down. Soon another man who wore a bright green G-string came out and gave Martha a lap dance. Martha pressed more ones into his G-String and she giggled like a schoolgirl. She looked right at me and whispered to the stripper. He swung on the vine over to where I sat and whirled my chair around, shaking his buttocks in my face! I struggled to breathe from the cologne that assaulted my senses. My cheeks felt instantly hot like I was having a hot flash. I was hot all right, but the dancer wasn't the reason. I was burning mad at Martha for sending that stripper over here.

El stood, waved a dollar bill and the stripper approached on his hands and knees, taking it between his teeth with a wink. As he turned to crawl away, Eleanor grabbed his G-string. Snap ... the entire room went wild when the man now stood completely naked! He covered himself and ran backstage. Within minutes, the doorman approached us and escorted us out of the club.

"Damn you, Eleanor. Why did you do that?"

"I just wanted to find out if he would take my AARP card," she giggled. "Your face is so red, Aggie. I think that young man shocked the hell out of you."

"He sure did." I breathed deeply of the night air and we strode toward the beach watching as the sun set, casting a yellow and orange glow. We meandered onto the patio where El pressed her face against the glass.

"Get over it, El. There's no way they'll let us back inside."

"Have I told you lately that you're a party pooper?"

"I think you pooped on your own party this time, grabbing that man's thong like that. What would Mr. Wilson say?"

"Well, you're not going to tell him, are you?"

"Of course not. I think it's best that we keep this whole evening on the down low."

El strolled toward the beach. "It would be nice to see the beach in the daylight."

I nodded, listening to the waves lap the shore. "It smells different than Lake Huron. You can almost smell the salt. I'm not sure I'm gonna like what it will do to my skin, though."

"The sun or the salt water?"

"Both. So El, what do you think about Bridgett trying to keep the maids' disappearances quiet?"

She sighed. "I don't know. We don't know for sure that she has. Nancy and Glenda were very forthcoming, but we just don't know how true what they said is. We can't question Bridgett about something like that."

My hands flew to my hips. "And why can't we?"

"Because, Aggie. She's hardly going to tell us the truth."

"I suppose you're right, but I'd sure love to put her on the hot seat again just to see what her reaction would be."

I was feeling my age tonight and was tired. I'd welcome my bed with open arms, but there was something about Eleanor that told me it wasn't going to happen anytime soon. She had that spark in her eye that I had grown accustomed to. My only hope was that I could lure her back to the retirement village without a fight.

From the corner of my eye, I caught sight of the shape of a man in the shadows. He was watching us! It was dark out now and we were vulnerable where we were. It was best to get moving before we became victims of a crime.

Chapter Eleven

I pulled Eleanor along as we wandered back to the street and hailed a cab to take us back to Sunny Brooke. It wasn't lost on me that somebody was following us, possibly the man in the shadows. I didn't want to make Eleanor nervous so I kept quiet about my suspicions.

En route we heard music that made you tap your foot and snap your fingers.

"Can't we stop here?" Eleanor whined. "I want to dance."

"Aren't you tired, old girl?"

"Heck, no! I'm a night owl."

I told the cab to stop and I paid the man. I had to hurry to keep up with Eleanor who exited the cab ahead of me. "Eleanor, slow down," I shouted. Boy, my hip was hurting me tonight.

Eleanor stopped and began swaying her hips to the music coming from a bar. "Let's go inside," Eleanor suggested.

I wasn't so sure that was such a great idea, but how do you say no to Eleanor? You don't. All you can do is hurry to catch up! I followed her into a bar named Nifty Fifty. Inside, the lights were lit low and a crowd was packed on the small dance floor. We wandered toward the bar and sat on two chairs at the mahogany counter. I pulled out a compact and lightly added powder to rid myself of my shine. Even at the age of seventy-two, my skin was still quite oily.

I gazed into the eyes of the bartender, a rather slender fellow with a smile the size of Texas. He was dressed respectfully in black slacks with a white ruffled shirt and black tie. Obviously this bar catered to the wealthier crowd as most the patrons were dressed to the nines, except us of course.

"What can I get you ladies?" the bartender asked.

I read his nametag. "Ted, I'd like a strawberry daiquiri. You, El?"

"An apple martini would do nicely."

"I'd be happy to buy the drink for you," a voice behind me offered.

I whirled around and stared into the dark eyes of a man with a hawk like nose, like the man who had shot our pilot from the plane. I was sure of it!

I tried not to panic, but I gulped. "Thanks, but I have it." I stared him down, noting his dark clothing and dress shoes on his feet. Was he the man who had been hiding in the shadows? Did he follow us here? But how? It was then that I remembered we had only gone a few blocks. It seemed implausible.

The man grinned, displaying a mouth full of teeth, one of which was gold. "Oh, come now. It's only a drink."

"Yeah, Aggie. Let him buy us the drink," Eleanor winked.

"Sorry, but we're taken and our men friends wouldn't like that." I kicked Eleanor under the bar.

Obviously catching on that I wasn't happy about the situation, El said, "Yeah, she's right."

"I don't see any men friends. Perhaps they aren't

here and you are all alone."

"I'm not alone." I thumbed in El's direction. "I'm with her."

El smiled. "Yes, and I'm with her."

"Hey, buddy," the bartender butted in. "The ladies don't want a drink from you. Push off or I'll call the bouncer over."

The man's eyes narrowed. "Fine. I'll see you ladies later."

He said it like it was a threat! When the bartender set our drinks down I passed him a twenty. "Thanks," I managed to choke out. "I don't like the looks of him."

"I'll agree with you on that one," the bartender said. "Be careful on your way home. If you like I'll have the bouncer run you home."

"Wow, you really know how to please your customers."

"My mom would have my ass if I let two old ladies get hurt on my watch," he winked.

"Old?" Eleanor said. "He must be talking about you and not me."

The bartender returned to work and El eyed me intently. "So what gives?"

"I think that man was the one who was planning to hijack the airplane we were on. He stared at me and I'm positive it was him."

"Like how? You barely saw him."

"He stared right at me and I remember that hawk-like nose of his."

"Are you suggesting he followed us to town?"

"Yes."

"How? Frank flew us to a different airport."

"Maybe somebody told him where we were dropped off."

"Who?"

"Those guys from Homeland Security." I frowned. "They didn't even believe our story about the pilot being shot."

"True, but it just seems like a strange coincidence, is all."

"We were shot at don't forget."

"Like I'd forget that! But Aggie, why do you think they'd want us dead?"

I screwed up my face. "How should I know? But either it was him or the jewelry thief."

El raised a hand. "I'm going with jewelry thief." She thanked the bartender who handed her a drink and she waited until he left before she said another word. "Why would the hijacker be looking for us?"

"How should I know? Unless..."

"Unless what, dear?"

"I found a packet that I thought Sheriff Peterson had given the pilot, but I'm not so sure now."

"You mean the one those guys from Homeland Security were asking about?"

"Yes." I wrung my hands. "There is no way Sheriff Peterson had given the pilot that packet."

"And why is that, Agnes?"

"Because it was filled with cash. Twenty-five thousand dollars to be exact."

El nearly fell over. "Holy cow! Now that's a lot of cash. I can't see the good sheriff having that much dough. And why give it to the pilot? Unless he was paying him to off you."

I narrowed my eyes. "You mean us. We're both a pain in his behind."

"Well, maybe the pilot was up to no good. I wonder what he intended to do with the money?"

"I'm not sure, but I also wonder why Homeland Security would want a packet of money."

"Maybe it's a payoff."

"Paying whom off is the question."

"It's definitely got something to do with illegal activity, but I wonder what kind."

Eleanor took a sip of her martini and then asked, "And where did you say this packet was now."

"I put it in a locker at Sunny Brooke."

"You what? You left it there? Why?"

"Oh, Bridgett was rushing us that day and I didn't have any pockets."

"We better get moving then and retrieve that packet before it goes missing."

I had completely forgotten that I had left it in the locker. What a bonehead I was. What if it wasn't there? *Oh God, Agnes. Pull yourself together!*

El and I finished our drinks and the bouncer, Marie, drove us back to Sunny Brooke. As it turns out, she was on the body building circuit and had more muscles than most men I know. We thanked her when she dropped us off and I ran in the door with Eleanor hot on my heels, all but ignoring Bridgett's voice asking us where we had been.

We found our way to the locker area and I pulled the string from around my neck that held the key, and hastily turned the lock. As I swung the locker open I yelled, "It's gone!" Not only the packet, but my purse!

Now, I hadn't had any valuables in that purse, but I had my ID and the packet containing twenty-five thousand in cash!

El's eyes bulged and she reached for her key to her locker and sure enough it was empty, too. "What in the hay?" she bellowed. "I have a mind to wring that Bridgett's neck."

I nodded in agreement and ran straight into Bridgett in the hallway. "Where are our belongings?" I demanded.

"Probably in your locker, dear."

"I already looked and it's empty."

"Maybe you took them to your room and forgot," Bridgett suggested.

"Maybe you robbed us," El bellowed. "Our clothes are even missing."

"And our ID."

"Hmm, nothing has ever happened like this before."

"Hogwash!" Eleanor spat. "You had two maids disappear into thin air and you keep a shotgun and shells on the premises."

I glared at her. "And now you'd like us to believe we simply forgot where we put our belongings."

"There's a thief running loose," Eleanor insisted. "And she's standing right here."

Bridgett fanned her face with her hand. "I'm not a thief. There is no way I'm responsible. There is no sense in crying wolf until you at least look in your room first."

"Fine, I'll look, but if I don't find my purse there I'm calling the sheriff."

Bridgett gasped at that. "Well—"

We didn't let her finish. We raced to our room and sure enough our purses weren't there. I called 911 and insisted they send Sheriff Calvin Peterson to the Sunny Brooke Retirement Village.

Chapter Twelve

There was a rap at the door ten minutes later and I let Sheriff Peterson inside with Bridgett following closely. After I settled myself on the couch, I neatly folded my hands in my lap and without any fanfare I said, "I believe Bridgett stole our belongings."

"I certainly did not," she huffed. "Maybe you didn't lock the locker properly."

"First I removed them and forgot and now I didn't lock the lock right!" I spat. "I know how to lock a damn lock."

El leaned against the wall. "You sure rushed us out of there, too."

"I needed the rooms cleaned."

"We're retired if you need to know," El informed her. "We never agreed to be slave labor."

Bridgett pursed her lips. "Sheriff Clem Peterson made the arrangements. Perhaps you should discuss that with him."

"I would," I began, "if he was here, but he's not, and now our belongings have been stolen, including our ID."

Calvin Peterson adjusted the waistband of his trousers. "This is a serious allegation, Agnes."

"All I know is we locked up our purses and clothes and now they are gone."

Peterson gazed out the window, his eyes narrowing

at the torrential downpour. “Are there any spare keys to the lockers, Bridgett?”

She threw her arms up. “Side with them, then.”

“I’m not siding with anyone. I just asked you a simple question.”

“Yes, the spare keys are downstairs.”

Bridgett led the way and we followed. When we were at the front counter, Andrew awaited with Putner and Palmer from Homeland Security! I ignored them and stared intently at Bridgett who unlocked and opened the door to access the counter area. She then reached under the counter and came back with a tin coffee can, rummaging through it.

My eyes widened. “You have to be kidding me. You keep the keys in a coffee can here?”

Bridgett raised a brow and from between gritted teeth. “Yes.”

“What’s going on?” Andrew asked.

“This woman told us to lock our things up and now they’re missing.”

“What’s missing?”

“Well, my clothes and purse.”

“If your purses have been missing all this time, how have you ladies been gallivanting around town?” Bridgett asked.

Eleanor muscled her way through the crowd. “Any self respecting lady keeps money in her bra. You outta know that.”

Bridgett rolled her eyes.

“So are the keys there or not?” I demanded. I felt sweat at the nape of my neck gather as Putner and Palmer stared at me. As of yet they stood there noting the scene with their sharp eyes.

Bridgett fumbled with keys that varied in size. "Oh, my!" she shouted. "They seem to be missing."

I stared from the door to the archway leading to the dining room and commons areas. "Who has access to this area?"

"Well, Jessica Bolf usually works back here."

"And where is Jessica now?" Sheriff Peterson asked.

"In her room, I suppose. She only works until seven."

"Give her a call. I'll need to question her."

Bridgett darted off and within five minutes, she returned with a lanky woman who had rollers in her hair, her face completely covered in cold cream.

"Do you know anything about the missing keys from the can?" the sheriff asked.

She shook her head. "No, I'm not in charge of handing keys out."

I pressed my hand to my chest. "Of course not dear, but has anyone been behind this counter that doesn't have a reason to be here?"

"Why, no. Miss Bridgett is very particular about that. Nobody is to be behind the counter but me or her."

I mused out loud. "So the counter isn't manned twenty-four seven, I assume. That means anyone could go back there."

"It's latched, see." Bridgett showed us the lock she had opened to go behind the counter.

I stared at the four-foot counter and assumed it was too high to simply jump over. "Who has a key to the counter area?"

"Just Jessica and me."

"And the maintenance man," Jessica pointed out.

"He's not here. He's home," Bridgett quickly added.

I leaned against the counter. "Does this man have a name?"

"Jamie Odell. He lives twenty minutes from Turtle Dune Beach. He'll be back in the morning."

I wiped at my brow. "When was the last time you saw the keys?"

She crossed her arms in a show of defiance. "I don't know."

El eyed Bridgett. "Yeah, right. Just fess up now before this gets more out of hand. Aggie had something quite valuable in her purse."

Putner interjected. "Like what?"

I shrugged. "Lipstick and my ID."

Andrew laughed. "The same lipstick from back home?"

I shook my head, embarrassed beyond words. Lord knows the batteries died long ago on that thing.

El puffed up her chest as she gazed at Putner. "What brings you boys by?"

Putner stepped forward. "We came to ask more questions."

I pulled at the collar to my shirt. "Like what?"

Palmer cut in. "About the packet from the airplane."

"I-I don't know what you mean."

"Yeah," El started. "We don't have any packet."

Andrew had a perplexed look on his face. "What kind of packet?"

"That's what we keep wondering," El spat. "They

keep carrying on about a packet, but won't tell us what's supposed to be in it."

Palmer's face reddened at that. "I know you have it. All you have to do is hand it over to us."

I bit my lip and said, "I don't have any packet. Search my room if you don't believe me."

Putner pulled out a folded paper. "That's why we're here. We have a search warrant."

El's hand flew to her chest. "Well then, I guess you boys had better search our room."

Andrew stopped me from leading the way. "Agnes told me about what happened on the plane. Have you found the dead pilot yet or is that a matter of national security?"

Putner clutched the paper. "As we told her back at the airport, there was no dead pilot found where they stopped."

"You couldn't have gone to the right airport, then," I insisted. "There had to be some evidence or blood splatter."

They shook their heads. "No," they chimed. "You ladies need a better story than would-be hijackers."

"Better story?" I asked.

"Yes, a better reason that you stole the packet."

"Now you're calling me a thief!" I shouted. "I don't even know what was in this imaginary packet." Putner stared at me like he was trying to scare me, but no way was that going to work. I wasn't about to tell him I found a packet of money in that airplane. "I'd like to see the search warrant."

"What for?" Palmer asked.

"I'd like to see some identification, too. How do I

know you really work for Homeland Security for sure?"

Badges were pulled out and Andrew examined them. "They look official, Agnes." Andrew took the papers Putner held, looked through them and with a snap of his wrist, he handed them back. "Show the gentlemen upstairs, Agnes."

I led the way, not worried that they would find anything, but more irritated by the whole situation. Once we were inside, Putner and Palmer rifled through drawers and our suitcases, tossing items onto the floor.

"Seriously, can't you be tidier? You don't need to trash the place."

The pair ignored me and continued until they went through all of our meager belongings. They then handed me a card. "Call us if you remember where you stashed the packet."

"I do remember something important about the would-be hijackers."

"Agnes, don't tell them anything. They won't believe a word you say," Eleanor scolded me.

Putner pulled out a notebook. "I'm listening."

"One of the men had a hawk-like nose, and when we were out earlier, I could have sworn I saw him. He might have followed us to Turtle Dune Beach."

Palmer raised a brow. "And how would he have found you here?"

"How should I know, but I'm sure it was him. He stared right at me back at the airport."

"How indeed," Eleanor spouted. "Maybe some little birdy is releasing information that should be kept quiet. We were shot at the other day. It could be the hijacker."

Putner's face reddened. "I'm sick of this whole hijacking theory. There is no proof that what you said happened, happened."

Andrew's brow furrowed. "What are you basing that on?"

"We didn't find the pilots body."

"The hijacker might have removed it."

"Mr. Hart, I have years of experience dealing with hijackers and this entire story is suspect. No offense, but your girlfriend is withholding valuable information. I can smell it."

"Fiddlesticks," El said. "You're just trying to railroad us. It wasn't only Agnes who saw the hijacker, we all did. He shot at the airplane!"

"Have you checked the surveillance tapes?" Andrew asked.

"The airport was a small one and they didn't have any."

"Someone else had to have been at that airport," I insisted.

"We checked that out and there wasn't anyone there."

"See?" Eleanor said. "Maybe because the hijackers took them out, too. No way was that airport as unattended as you are trying to say."

Putner went for the door and he whipped it open to a rattled Dorothy Alton, who stood there gripping a tattered tissue. "I-I'm not interrupting, am I?"

"Not at all, dear," I said and led her into the room, watching in amusement as Palmer and Putner tripped from the room over Dorothy's suitcase. That will teach them.

I shut the door and led Dorothy to the couch while

Eleanor poured a glass of wine for her. As the wine glass was pressed into Dorothy's hand, she drank it down in one gulp.

"What's wrong, Dorothy?"

"It's Frank. He threw me out," she wailed. "H-He thinks I was cheating on him with Eugene Bragsworth, but I swear that's not the truth."

"Have you checked the locker for your belongings, Dorothy?"

She nodded. "They were gone. I thought Frank took them."

"I don't think so, because our belongings disappeared from the lockers, too," I informed her.

"With my purse missing I don't have a dime. Even if I wanted to go back home I couldn't. Frank has really lost it this time. No way will he take me back."

Eleanor poured herself a glass of wine and gulped it down. "Nonsense. That man is in love with you, Dorothy. You have been married for far too long to just throw it all away now."

"I-I know, but what can I do?"

"I'm going to help you, old girl. If you trust me, that is," El said. "You do know I was only kidding when I flirted with Frank in the past. I just liked to rile you up, is all."

"I guess, but what if you can't help and Frank is done with me for good?"

"Don't worry, Dorothy," I said. "I promise we won't rest until you're back with Frank."

Eleanor opened the bedroom door. "Get some rest, Dorothy. We'll plot tomorrow."

Dorothy dragged her feet all the way to the bedroom and closed the door behind her. El then joined her inside leaving Andrew and me alone. "Poor dear," I commented and then brought Andrew up to speed about why Frank was so mad at Dorothy.

Andrew nodded. "I don't blame Frank for being mad. I would be mad, too, if someone was trying to put the moves on you."

"That's silly. No way would I ever put myself into that type of situation. That Bragsworth was really wining and dining Dorothy, but why exactly?"

"Perhaps he's lonely."

"He was eyeing up her jewelry and there is a jewelry thief in town. El and I even encountered him in a shop downtown. I wonder if Bragsworth is the person responsible for the robberies?"

"Romancing a married woman isn't against the law, you know. What, besides your snoopy nature, has you thinking this Bragsworth could be responsible?"

"It's a feeling I have."

"You're a sleuth. You need to focus on the facts and you simply have no facts to support your assumption. And what about this packet those guys from Homeland Security keep going on about?"

I avoided his eyes. "How would I know?"

Andrew lifted my chin. "What gives? I know you too well, Agnes."

I sighed. "Well, I found a packet on the airplane."

"Did you open it?"

"Yes. It had twenty-five thousand dollars inside."

"Where is the money now?"

"Gone. It was inside my purse when it was stolen."

"So we have us a thief here then. Do you think

Bridgett is really responsible?"

"I'm not sure, but she gets my vote."

He shook his head at me. "Putner and Palmer sure acted like something besides money was inside that packet."

"I know. I wonder if there were two packets. Maybe the pilot had the other one."

"I guess we'll never know unless we get your purse back. Tomorrow we'll tear this place apart looking for it. I can't believe your purses were pilfered from a locked locker. Somebody has to know something."

"I keep hoping."

Andrew excused himself, telling me he'd try to reason with Frank. Without anywhere to sleep, I laid down on the couch, which was quite soft, and drifted off instantly.

Chapter Thirteen

I awoke to the sound of birds chirping and a woman screaming. Bolting toward the patio door, I saw a grey-haired woman screaming at the top of her lungs, pointing toward the swamp.

Eleanor and Dorothy surfaced from the bedroom, still dressed in what they wore yesterday. We made our way outside, trudging through the high grass to where the woman was standing. She gripped a shoe to her ample bosom.

"What's all the hoopla about?" I asked the woman.

"He's gone. Oh God, he's gone."

"Who is?"

"Eugene Bragsworth. He told me last night he was going to take a walk to clear his head and he never came back," she sobbed.

"What makes you think he came out here?"

"He left via his patio door and here's his shoe." She handed me an oxford shoe. "It's his. He was wearing it the last time I saw him."

"I'm sorry. I didn't catch your name."

"Eunice Bragsworth."

"Are you related to Eugene?"

"He's my husband." She then glared at Dorothy. "It's all your fault, you harlot. You were putting the moves on my husband."

Dorothy's eyes widened. "That's not how it went.

We were just friends."

"Your husband nearly killed my Eugene. Maybe he came back to finish the job."

"N-No, my Frank wouldn't do that. Plus, he threw me out."

"That doesn't mean anything."

I interrupted the ladies. "So we have another shoe near the swamp."

"I wonder if a gator got him," Eleanor put in. "Just like what happened to the maids."

"I doubt it, El. I'm not so sold on that idea."

Eunice folded her arms. "All I know is that my husband is missing because of this woman."

I rolled my eyes. This doesn't make a lick of sense. Bridgett came running forward in a panicked state. "What's happened?"

"My Eugene is missing. I found his shoe," Eunice informed her. "Maybe that man who nearly killed him last night came back to finish the job and dumped his body for the gators."

"My Frank isn't a murderer," Dorothy insisted.

"Where was he last night?"

"I don't know. I told you he threw me out."

"There's a murderer loose around here is all I know," Eunice cried. "My husband would never hurt a flea."

El interrupted her. "Nope. He just romanced other men's wives."

"It wasn't my Eugene. It was that woman." She pointed at Dorothy, who quivered.

"I suppose you better call the sheriff, Bridgett. If anything, Eugene is missing."

"Maybe the alligators got him like the maids," Bridgett suggested.

"I'm about sick of that theory, but one thing is for certain. Frank couldn't have done anything untoward to Eugene. He's a reasonable man."

"He did try and shoot him yesterday," Bridgett reminded me.

Bridgett pulled her cell phone out and dialed 911 to report Eugene Bragsworth missing. Once she hung up she suggested, "We should go inside before another alligator comes along."

"Or snakes," I added. Lord knows Florida had its share of poisonous snakes and I'd rather not meet one first hand.

We congregated in the commons room that had leather sofas and recliner chairs. Along one wall there was a bookshelf packed with books and along the other was a large screen television affixed to the wall. Pool tables also encompassed the room.

Sheriff Peterson came into the room, smoothing his hair back with a swipe of his meaty hand. "When was the last time any of you saw Eugene Bragsworth?"

I put my hand in the air. "The last time I saw him was right after Frank nearly shot him. He was in his room at the time." Ouch, that didn't sound good for Frank at all.

"What?" Peterson bellowed. "Why wasn't I called?"

"It was nothing, really," Bridgett said. "He only shot Bragsworth's door frame." She glared at me. "I'm sure the gators got him."

Eunice burst into tears. "Oh, no. My poor Eugene

being chomped to bits by gators!"

"Was that the last time any of you saw Eugene?"

The crowd nodded except for Eunice, who informed the sheriff that Eugene hadn't returned from a walk to clear his head.

"Where is this Frank?" Peterson asked.

Everyone looked at Dorothy, who shrugged. "He threw me out. I told you that," she yelled at nobody in particular. "I slept in Agnes' and Eleanor's room." She smacked her lips. "Maybe Mr. Wilson knows where he is. I'm sure they were together last night."

"My boyfriend, Andrew Hart, was going to look for Frank last night, too. Maybe they were together."

Frank appeared at the door and Dorothy ran to him, but he pushed her back. "I'm here to confess."

Gasps split the air. "What are you confessing to, Frank?" I asked.

"I almost shot Bragsworth. What did you think? When I saw the sheriff's car I figured I might as well fess up."

"The sheriff is here about the disappearance of Bragsworth," I informed him.

The sheriff stepped forward. "I appreciate your help, Agnes, but please let me ask the questions."

"Where were you last night, Frank?" Peterson asked.

"I threw that cheating wife of mine out and then I went for a walk to clear my head."

"Did Mr. Wilson go with you?" I couldn't help but ask.

"Agnes Barton. Would you please butt out," Peterson bellowed.

"I was just wondering, is all."

"Yeah," Eleanor said. "You can't blame her for asking questions. It's what we do. We're senior snoops."

Peterson adjusted his waistband. "I know, but I said no snooping on my watch, remember? I have been quite tolerant. The least you ladies could do is let me lead this investigation."

"Fine," I spouted.

"Did anyone accompany you on this walk?"

"Nope. I went alone."

"So you ran across Bragsworth and had words with him?"

"He never said that," I spat. Peterson was certainly being the bad cop.

"No. I never ran into anyone. I walked outside and sat in the gazebo listening in enjoyment to the frogs croaking up a storm," Frank clarified. "I'm glad I didn't run into that man."

Peterson's eyes narrowed. "Why is that? Because you would have finished the job?"

"How would I know? I was still steamed, but I blame my wife more than him."

Dorothy wrung her hands. "Oh, Frank, nothing happened."

"You sure traipsed around enough with the man. For all I know, you're lying to me now." He shook his head. "I just don't trust you anymore, Dorothy. I can't bear the thought of you with that man."

"I'd like you to come down to the station for more questioning," Peterson said.

"And what for? You haven't even established something untoward might have happened to Bragsworth.

Maybe he took off after his encounter with Frank."

"No, I saw him after that," Eunice assured us. "He didn't say a word to me about wanting to leave and he'd never leave without telling me."

I faced Eunice. "Where have you been hiding? We haven't seen you before today."

"I was visiting my daughter in Tampa and I came back early last night. That's when I found Eugene's door shot to bits."

"Did you discuss it?"

"Yes, he told me," pointing at Dorothy, "The harlot was trying to get him into the sack."

Dorothy gasped. "I was not! He was the aggressor. He kept kissing my hand."

Eleanor nodded. "Aggie and I saw him doing that on more than one occasion. We even followed Bragsworth and Dorothy to Clammy's the other day."

"Y-You what?" Dorothy's face reddened. "You were watching us the whole time?"

El rolled back on her heels. "Yup, he was all over you like cheap cologne."

"Trollop!" Frank yelled. "I want a divorce."

Tears poured down Dorothy's face. "I didn't mean for anything to happen and it didn't! But when you shot that door frame, I realized it went too far," she sniveled.

"Arrest me, Sheriff, before I kill my wife."

I bit down on my knuckle. "Oh, you don't mean that Frank."

"But I do. She's trying to cover up her evil deeds again, just like in 1972."

My eyes widened. "1972?"

"She was running around with Jack Winston!"

"Surely you jest. Not that sex fiend. You weren't the one he was cheating on his wife with?"

"No, we were just friends. I told Frank that like a thousand times, but he wouldn't believe me and neither did his wife. He had an affair with Elsie Bradford."

A smile split El's face. "Not the leader of the social circles in East Tawas?"

"One and the same. She'll deny it, of course, but I saw them skinny dipping in Lake Huron."

"And this happened in 1972?"

"Yes."

El laughed. "I always knew she couldn't be that perfect, and after the way she looks down her nose at everyone who has a man or a life."

Sheriff Peterson shook his head. "Come along, Frank."

"Hey, now. For one thing it hasn't been established that Eugene Bragsworth was murdered. All we have is a shoe by the swamp."

"He disappeared into thin air just like the maids," Bridgett pointed out. "Maybe you should search the swamp."

Peterson rubbed the back of his neck. "After we do a thorough search of the rooms and grounds."

I handed Eugene's oxford shoe to the sheriff. With a curt nod he radioed for more officers. Within ten minutes the place was swarming with cops. I followed Peterson to Bragsworth's room and as we entered, the place was in disarray. Drawers had been thrown open and the contents scattered on the floor.

"Oh, my," Eunice cried. "Someone must have come in here when we were in the commons room."

"It wasn't like this before?" I asked.

"Why, no."

I stared down at the trashcan and found a knitted cap and, picking it up, I saw it was a ski mask! I handed it to the sheriff who lifted a brow. "What's this, Agnes?"

"It's a ski mask. Maybe Eugene Bragsworth is the jewelry thief."

"Not possible," Dorothy called from the doorway. "I told you I was with him the whole time when Nina's was robbed."

"And you're positive?" I asked.

"Yes, quite."

Disregarding what she said, I continued. "This Eugene Bragsworth could be the jewelry thief and his supposed disappearance a smoke screen."

"And the trashed up room, Aggie?" El asked.

"Deliberately done to throw us off the trail."

Peterson looked about ready to swallow his tongue. "We don't know that for sure, but I'll take this mask and ask Julie from Julie's Jewels if it looks like the mask the robber wore." He cleared his throat. "Until then, please excuse us and go back to your room."

"Wh-What?"

"This is official police business and you're standing in a potential crime scene. So out, the lot of you."

We left the room and congregated downstairs in the commons room again. Eunice was seated next to Frank and patted his hand affectionately. "I'm sorry I blamed you for my husband's disappearance. I guess I just don't know what to think." She bowed her head. "I had hoped Eugene had changed his ways. I always knew he was a louse, but this just takes the cake. Trying to romance your wife like that."

"Well, I-I—"

"Take your hands off my husband," Dorothy spat. With that she elbowed her way between El and me and snatched Eunice's hand from Frank. She pushed back and Dorothy fell right on her butt.

El puffed up her chest. "Get away from Frank, you hussy."

"Stop it, ladies. There is plenty of Frank to go around," he snickered.

Mr. Wilson took that moment to shuffle forward in this walker. "Ladies, stop before you send this old boy into cardiac arrest."

I glanced over at the frail looking Mr. Wilson and wondered whom he was talking about — Frank or him. From the way El's eyes glazed over I figured it was him. "Mr. Wilson," El began. "I'll stand for no more wandering. The retired school teacher was enough."

"Oh, and where did you go last night? Strip club from what I heard. You ripped a G-string off a stripper."

"I-I," she turned toward me. "Tell him, Aggie."

I raised my hands. "Tell him what, that you're incorrigible beyond repair." I fell silent for a moment, noticing Andrew standing in the doorway with a raised brow. "Who told you that, Wilson?"

Musical laughter from behind Andrew told me who. Martha strode forward, her jungle print shirt and pants hugging her curves.

Chapter Fourteen

I raised a brow. "Martha. How kind of you to join the party. I'd ask where you've been, but I'm not sure I care to know."

"Well, the male strippers show for one. I'm still reeling over Eleanor's antics. It's not every day you see two old ladies ousted from the event of the season," she winked. "You didn't think I was planning to hang out at the old folk's home, did you?"

"It's a retirement village, Martha," I corrected her. "And it's been quite eventful around here lately."

Martha hung her head. "I suppose you're planning to give me all the juicy details, but it will have to wait. I'm famished and I could use a change of clothes."

"You mean you own something besides animal print?" I said in mock outrage.

"Very funny, Mother."

I'd press her for more details, but I figured what's the use? She's old enough to make her own mistakes without me pointing them out. "I'd be happy to show you to my room so you can....," I took a whiff of the less than fresh fragrance of Martha, "Shower."

Dorothy waltzed over to where I stood. "I'll go along, too. I've had too much excitement for one day."

El motioned over to Eunice. "Are you sure you want to go now, Dorothy."

Frank was smiling at Eunice who still sat next to

him, apparently liking the attention. I thought that a bit strange considering she had just carried on about her husband's disappearance. She certainly changed her tune quick.

Dorothy looked over at Frank and then said, "Yes. There's nobody here that I want to talk to."

Frank still had his sights on Eunice, and El volunteered to stay behind, but Dorothy wasn't having it. "Come along, Eleanor."

"But Dorothy—"

"But what? A divorce will be the best thing I've done in years. There's plenty of other fish in the sea."

I rolled my eyes. How much worse could it get?

"Don't worry. I'll keep an eye on Frank," Andrew assured us. "Strippers, eh? If I knew you'd liked things like that I'd go out and buy a G-string myself," he winked.

As I made for the door Andrew swatted my rear. "Behave yourself," I called over my shoulder.

Walking toward our rooms, Dorothy dabbed at her eyes with her sleeve. "It's hopeless. I've lost Frank for good."

"Nonsense. He's probably just trying to make you mad."

"Yeah," Eleanor said. "That man is crazy about you."

"Or just plain crazy," Martha added.

"That will be enough out of you, Martha. Don't you see Dorothy's upset?"

She shrugged. "So what gives?"

I brought Martha up to speed on what had been happening, the jewelry thief, our stolen purses, and the missing Eugene Bragsworth.

"My," Martha began, "you girls sure have been busy. And to think all I have been doing is partying with men on the beach."

Eleanor pouted. "Lucky duck. I have yet to even make it to the beach."

I eyed Eleanor's sad face. "We'll go later if that makes you happy, Eleanor. I'd hate to deprive you."

Eleanor rubbed her hands together. "I can't wait."

When we passed Bragsworth's room, Sheriff Peterson stood there with a black garbage bag full of who knows what.

"Did you find anything?"

"Agnes, I'm handling the investigation, remember? It's no wonder my brother sent you to Florida for the winter."

Eleanor whizzed past him. "Because we earned the trip is why."

"I'd be happy to pay you ladies to go back to Michigan."

"Good try, but no. That's not going to fly. We'll keep an eye out for Eugene. Who knows, maybe he'll come back. Or do you believe he's really missing?"

"It's too early to tell, but if he isn't back by morning we'll be searching the swamp." He buttoned his lips after that and left with his deputies.

I led the way back to our room and once we were inside, Martha made a beeline for the shower, which I was happy about.

"What was that fragrance Martha was wearing?" El asked. "Three days of sweat?"

"I'd rather not know. So that was odd, Eunice flirting with Frank."

"Yes, considering she just about accused him of murdering her husband."

"My Frank wouldn't do a thing like that."

I opened my curtains and gazed outside. There was a group of ten out back looking toward the swamp. "Looks like some ambulance chasers are outside."

El joined me. "Yes. We really need to meet more of the locals around here. I'd love to hear their take on the whole disappearance. Maybe they know something Bridgett isn't willing to tell us."

"True, El, but I wonder if they are all going to be as tight lipped. I can't imagine they want the retirement village to look bad considering they live here."

"Why would anyone willingly live somewhere that people keep turning up missing?" Martha said from the bathroom door. She was wrapped in a towel with another one wrapped around her head.

"There has to be a reason. I just wish we knew more about Bridgett and the retirement village. I mean, why would anyone want to stay somewhere where there is a swamp in the backyard?"

Martha dressed quietly in the corner, donning cutoff jeans and a white tee, the most respectable clothing I have seen her wear thus far. She tossed her towels into the linen bag and smirked. "I hope the cleaning ladies pick up those towels soon. I just hate the smell of musty towels."

My brow arched. "Oh, did I forget to tell you? We are the cleaning ladies."

"Yuck, count me out."

I smiled affectionately. "Aw, come on. It won't be

so bad for someone young like you."

"I'm forty, Mother, not twenty-four."

I rolled my eyes. Martha certainly didn't act anywhere near forty. My thoughts then traveled to Sophia and I gave her a quick call, but it went straight to the answering machine. I frowned, lost in thought. I hoped the poor dear wasn't too sick. Could El be right that she might be p— *Stop it Agnes. It's none of your business.*

El tapped her fingernails on the table until I looked up. "What?"

"You know what. I want to go to the beach. You promised."

"And so I did. Oh, why not."

Martha perked up. "What about the cleaning gig?"

"It can wait until we come back."

El loaded her bag with towels, tanning lotion, and changed into her swimsuit, a pink one piece with a huge yellow flower centered on it. I went into the bathroom and donned a blue one piece that had a skirt for the bottom. I hoped it would at least hide some of my rolls. I'm not as confident as Eleanor. I laughed. I don't think anyone is.

We high-tailed it down the stairs, boarding the bus that would take us to town. Darcy was at the helm and when I asked her why, she just shrugged.

As she shifted the bus into gear she announced, "Hold on, ladies." The bus jetted ahead, leaving a smoke trail behind and scattering stones.

I sat right behind Darcy. "How long have you worked here, Darcy?"

Keeping her eyes on the road she answered, "Long enough."

I leaned forward in my seat. "Long enough to know the real reason the maids disappeared?"

She choked at that. "I'm not sure anyone knows the real reason for sure. Bridgett thinks the gators got them. That might be the truth."

Here we go again with the gators. "One maid, maybe, not two."

"Stranger things have happened in this town."

"Like what?"

"Shark attacks for one. Two sisters just last month."

El's eyes bulged. "Really? I thought sharks didn't attack people on purpose, that they might think that they are a seal or something."

"That's true, Miss Eleanor, most of the time. Don't worry about it, though. I promise you'll have a great time at the beach. There's plenty of eye candy there."

El slapped her leg. "That's what I'm talking about, men in their skivvies."

I rolled my eyes. "What about Mr. Wilson?"

"What about him? He's not attached to my hip, you know. Andrew sure seems to make himself scarce. Trouble in paradise?"

"No. He stayed behind to keep Frank out of mischief."

"Did you notice that Frank is hearing much better lately?"

"Maybe he's keeping his hearing aid turned up."

"What's that?" Dorothy asked.

I smiled at her. "Oh, nothing, dear. Let's just forget about the men and have a nice day on the beach."

She nodded, glancing out the window, either lost in thought or dismissing the mention of Frank altogether. I hoped it was the latter. Dorothy needed to get her predicament off her mind. There had to be a way to reunite Frank and Dorothy. I couldn't imagine this going on for too long unless Eunice didn't back off. I had yet to decide what Eunice is up to. She couldn't be looking for another husband so quick. *Lord knows her husband has not been missing that long*, I thought.

The bus rumbled to a stop with the loud whoosh of the air brakes. We thanked Darcy and exited the bus, listening with pleasure to the Cuban music playing. When we walked onto the beach, hot sand packed itself into my sandals. "Ouch!"

"It sure is hot out here," Eleanor whined as she trudged through the sand.

We all gasped when we spotted the crystal clear water. Sailboats were aplenty and jet ski's whizzed past. Excited screams of children carried over to us as they were making their sand castles that resembled mansions! Boy, these Florida kids sure had some artistic skills.

I pulled out a blanket and we plopped down. "This sure is beautiful."

"It sure is, Aggie," El said. "I could die right here."

"I hope not! Geez, Eleanor, what a thing to say."

"It sure isn't anything like Lake Huron. The water is so clear and blue," she sighed.

"I rather like my Lake Huron. I sure miss the gang back home."

El's face wrinkled up. "Like who, Sheriff Peterson?"

"Who knew he'd have an equally annoying brother."

Dorothy squirted the sun tan lotion and applied it to her arm. "He's not annoying; he just doesn't want you snooping."

El scoffed. "That's like telling a leopard to change its spots."

"True, but I wished he had taken Frank in for questioning."

I took the tanning lotion from Dorothy. "Why?

"Because he'd be out of the clutches of *that woman*."

I shielded my eyes from the sun. "You can't be thinking Frank would really stray on you like that."

"Well, he thinks I did and that's all it takes for some men. Maybe my granddaughter will let me stay with her when I get back home."

I couldn't imagine poor Sally Alton would want Dorothy staying with her. Sally had told me more than once her grandparents' bickering got on her nerves. I can't imagine what living with Dorothy would be like on a daily basis, one of the reasons I needed to help her get back with Frank. El and I lived in cramped quarters as it was.

I changed the subject. "Let's test the water out and remember to be on the lookout for jellyfish. You don't want to be stung by one of those."

We got up and wandered toward the water and when I stepped into it, I was surprised at how warm it was. "Wow, what a great feeling."

"Much better than cold Lake Huron," El said.

"Why do you keep downing Lake Huron? I thought you loved it. You do live on the lake."

El wrinkled her nose. "I love my house on the lake,

but I sure love Florida. Maybe we should move here."

I waded into the water until I was up to my knees. "I think not. It's winter here now so the temperature isn't that bad. You wouldn't last one summer here."

"Plus there aren't any hurricanes in Michigan," Dorothy added.

El fell silent and looked down toward her toes in wonder as she walked toward me. "Look, Aggie. Fish."

Schools of fish swam past and in that moment, I could almost agree that Florida wouldn't be a half bad place to live. It was like a whole new world for us here.

A large wave appeared straight ahead of us and we toppled over as it crashed to shore. When it had passed, both El and I sputtered. "Wow! That was some wave."

"It sure was. Look at the surfers!"

Sure enough, surfers paddled their way as another wave rolled up. One made for the wave and jumped on his yellow surfboard, riding the wave to where we stood. I eyed the surfer in shock. He was only about ten!

"Great ride," the boy shouted as he paddled back out.

"These children sure have plenty of fun things to do here in Florida." I stared at Eleanor and noticed she was turning pink. "Hey, El. We better get out of the sun before you turn into a lobster."

"Aw, Aggie. I want to stay in the water."

"Listen to my mom," Martha pointed toward the beach. "Get out of the water."

"Geez, you girls aren't any fun."

We wandered back to the beach and gathered our things, making way for a beachside ice cream stand. It was white and had room only for one person to stand in, with the name Tootsie scrawled in neon pink lettering. I breathed in deeply, enjoying the fragrances of twenty-eight flavors and waffle cones.

"Can I help you ladies?" a fresh-faced girl asked. Her dazzling smile reminded me a little of my granddaughter, Sophia. Her thin frame was covered with a white apron smeared with chocolate and strawberry syrup covering her hot pink bikini underneath.

"Sure. I'd love chocolate marshmallow on a waffle cone." I beamed at the girl, noting her deep dimples.

"Right away." She pushed a strand of her blond hair back and scooped the ice cream that was located in a sliding freezer.

The other girls ordered and soon we all had a waffle cone in hand and sat at a table under a huge yellow umbrella. Eleanor slurped at her ice cream and winced a little. "I guess I am a little burnt."

"You do have fair skin. That's what I was trying to tell you."

"Okay, Mom," she snickered. "I just love the beach. Maybe we should have come in the evening."

"Good idea for next time," I said. "I suppose we should be heading back soon if we are to question the residents of Sunny Brooke."

"Does that include me?" Martha asked.

"It sure does. It won't kill you to hang out with the old folks."

"It's not that. I was hoping to be included, is all. I had such great fun on your last case."

"Don't remind me about that one. El and I were almost toast."

El went to lick her cone again and the ice cream plopped on her foot. "Oh, darn. I lost my ice cream."

I handed her a napkin and then we left in search of the bus that was parked on the main drag. We boarded and Darcy skidded back onto the highway. She swerved to miss tourists crossing the road and passed a Mack truck!

"Hey!" I yelled. "Slow down, would ya?"

"Yeah," Eleanor added. "You trying to give us a heart attack?"

"Sorry, tight schedule. I better get back to the kitchen before Mr. Wilson makes tuna casserole again for lunch."

I smiled to myself. Oh, yeah, Mr. Wilson's dreaded specialty. It was good, but not something you'd want for lunch everyday. Although if you asked El, she'd tell you she'd eat it everyday. I hoped she was talking about the casserole and not something else.

When we arrived, the sheriff was long gone. Now maybe we could do a little digging without him interfering. I ran straight into Andrew right inside the archway. "Hey, there, gorgeous. Where have you been hiding?" he asked smiling.

"The beach."

Upon seeing Eleanor's reddened skin he said, "Ah, I see."

I stared straight ahead and ran toward Eugene Bragsworth. "Hey, what do you think you were doing scaring us all half to death?"

Bragsworth turned and smiled. "You must also think I'm my brother, Eugene. I'm Ernie Bragsworth."

"But you look just like your brother."

"He sure does," Dorothy gushed.

I gave Dorothy a hard stare.

"I get that all the time. We're twins."

I shook my head. So Eugene has a twin brother? The wheels were turning, but I had to still them. "I imagine you're here about your brother's disappearance."

"Yes, I'm quite shocked. Eugene isn't the type of man to just disappear into thin air. I also can't see him going anywhere near a swamp. He's afraid of snakes."

"Me, too," Eleanor said as she extended a hand to shake. "I'm Eleanor Mason."

I wanted to give her a kick. "So what gives? Do you live around here?"

"Why no, dear lady. I live in Miami, but when I heard my brother was missing I hopped a plane to get here post haste. We need to do an extensive search here first and then check out that swamp just in case he went in there, although I think the notion is ludicrous."

I stared at the man. He certainly looked exactly like Eugene. "I'd be happy to help, Bragsworth. I'm Agnes Barton and a sleuth of sorts."

"Well, then, I'm in good hands. I'd rather not have the sheriff more involved if at all possible."

"And why is that?"

"Because, dear lady, I have had my fair share of run-ins with Sheriff Peterson in the past and I'd rather not endure any more.

"I suppose that make sense." It kinda was my sentiment, although I sure wanted to hear if the ski mask found in Bragsworth's room was the same one used by the jewelry thief — fat chance Peterson giving us the down low about that one. El and I had best high-tail it down to Julie's Jewels to find out tomorrow.

Chapter Fifteen

Dorothy, El, and I waited for Bragsworth in the hallway outside Eugene's room. He apparently had to do his own search of the room without us.

"What do you think he's up to?" El asked.

"Who knows, but I'm damn sure gonna find out."

I rapped on the door until Ernie answered with a towel wrapped around his waist, a wicked grin on his face. "Sorry, ladies. I thought I might as well take a quick shower. I'm sure my brother wouldn't mind me utilizing his room while I'm here."

"Are you sure you're not Eugene Bragsworth?"

"I'm positive. He's a cad, whereas I am not. Give me ten more minutes and I'll join you ladies." With that, he closed the door.

"Well, well," Bridgett said from behind us. "I guess I can't count on you ladies cleaning anytime soon. I have half a mind to call Clem Peterson back in East Tawas and tell him the deal is off."

El stepped forward. "No, you just have half a mind."

I pulled El back. "She means we'll clean the rooms later."

Bridgett sashayed her way up the hallway and disappeared into one of the rooms.

"El, be careful. That woman might send us packing and then what would we do?"

"Live at the beach."

"With what? Our purses are missing, or did you forget?"

El puffed her chest up. "My memory is sharp as a tack."

"Where is that daughter of yours?" Dorothy asked me.

I glanced around and shrugged. "Who knows, but I want get into Bragsworth's room. I'm sure we might find something of interest."

"Maybe our purses," El said. "That is, if Bridgett didn't take them."

I leaned against the wall. "She had more of an opportunity, but we need to keep our options open. It could be anybody."

"We better find them and soon before those fellas from Homeland Security come back."

"There is something not right about those guys," I observed.

"Besides accusing us of having a mysterious package?"

"Yes. How would the man with the hawk nose have found us if he wasn't told by Putner and Palmer where we were?"

"Yeah, but how did they find out where we went? We only gave them our addresses in Michigan."

"They must have seen Sheriff Peterson pick us up. Remember we were picked up with the Sunny Brooke Retirement Village bus. All they had to do was tell Mr. Hawk Nose where we went."

I swallowed hard. "If he found out we were in Turtle Dune Beach then—"

"He could come here!" El bit down on her knuckles. "Oh, my! He knows where we are!"

My heart thudded against my chest. "Calm down, now. We don't know that. He offered to buy us a drink, is all."

"Oh, Aggie! Wh-What if he comes here looking for us? We'll be goners!"

"You need to calm down, El. First things first. We need to get into that room."

Bragsworth surfaced and locked the door behind him. "Sorry I took so long, ladies."

I peered toward the door. "Yeah. What took you so long?"

El laughed, her whole belly shaking. "What are you hiding in there?"

I gave El a stern look. "Nobody we know I hope."

Ernie folded his arms. "I'm sorry. I'm at a loss here."

"You know, like that your brother is hiding out."

"And why would he do that?"

I fingered a loose string on my blouse. "Oh, I don't know. Maybe there is a good reason he's hiding out."

"Yeah," Dorothy said. "They found a ski mask in his room earlier."

I wanted to give Dorothy a kick.

"Do tell? And why would my brother have a ski mask in his room?"

I stared off in the distance. "Because he might be a jewelry thief."

Dorothy scoffed. "I told you I was with him the whole time the other day in town."

El's face contorted. "Then why would he have a ski

mask in his room?"

"He gets cold sometimes," Dorothy whispered. "He told me as much."

"This is Florida, Dorothy," I spat.

Dorothy shuffled her feet. "How do I know? It's just something he mentioned."

"Did my brother mention anything else, like he was planning to take a trip?"

"Well, no." Dorothy began, "But he did say he was thinking about moving on. I thought he meant with me."

I rolled my eyes. "You're a married woman! How could you be taking a word that man said to you without a grain of salt? He's a no good wife stealer."

"You're getting all carried away. It doesn't matter anymore. When I saw Frank with the shotgun I knew I had gone too far. But I guess it doesn't matter anymore because Frank threw me out."

"Wow. My brother has been very busy indeed."

"Yes, but it's still a mystery why he'd suddenly take off."

"You girls think everything is a mystery. The only mystery I see is what I'll have to do to get Frank back. He seems taken with Bragsworth's wife."

"Wife?" Ernie said shocked. "You mean Eunice is here?"

What an odd thing to say. Was Eunice even Eugene's wife? And what about Ernie? Was he the real deal? Something about his quick appearance from Miami had me wondering like he had already known his brother went missing beforehand. Not much else I could do but see how it all plays out.

I changed the subject. "So where do we look first?"

Ernie rubbed a hand over his grey head. "Let's check every room and every closet. If he's here, we'll find him."

We went in search of Eugene knocking on doors, but we were turned away on every occasion until the last door. A woman with flowing blond hair led us inside. "Jack, they're here about the missing guy."

He swiveled his chair to face us and my mouth slacked open. "Jack Winston," I exclaimed. "How? What? Are you d-doing here?"

"Trying to escape the winter like you, I expect," he answered motioning to Eleanor. "I see you brought fish lady."

Jack Winston was my age and dated younger women like the one who answered the door. She batted her false eyelashes at me when I stared at her. "How old are you?"

"Twenty-three. Why?"

I admired the girl's fit physique. She was dressed in white shorts with a pink tank top displaying a fair amount of cleavage. "Oh, no reason."

"You're way too young for the likes of him," Eleanor exclaimed. "What would your mother think?"

She fidgeted with a strand of her hair. "Well, she introduced us. Jack's not so bad when you get used to him."

Jack's dark hair blew from the oscillating fan that was positioned on his desk and he pulled out a toothpick from his pocket, proceeding to pick at his teeth. Indicating Ernie, he offered, "I see you found Bragsworth."

"No, sir. I'm Eugene's brother, Ernie."

"I see. Well, you must be twins then. I'd be careful with these two," motioning toward El and me. "They are a bit touched in the head."

El balled up her fist. "Be careful, Jack. Remember what happened the last time we met. I believe you were stuck in a lawn chair."

"No dear, the last time we saw him, he was being arrested for assaulting a police officer."

"Oh, at Rosa Lee Hill's p—"

"Barbeque you mean." I didn't care to talk about Rosa Lee's medicinal crop. She had turned over an new leaf. "She now sells potpourri."

"Of course. I had forgotten that, Aggie," El said.

Jack's eyes were bloodshot red. "Why are you two here?"

"I was wondering if you saw Eugene Bragsworth the night he disappeared."

"He was walking out back."

"Toward the swamp?"

"Yes, there's one out there. Bridgett sure left that one out of the brochure, but not much I can do about it now."

El rested her hand against the table. "Why is that? Surely you could have left."

"Not without losing my deposit. I signed a lease. If I tried to leave before spring, she pockets twenty-five thousand in cash."

El's eyes lit up. "Wow, that's a lot of dough."

I was very interested now in what Jack had to say. "So you signed the lease before you came here?"

"Yes, and I had to wire her the money before I

came." He tossed the brochure toward me. "She sent me this."

I glanced at the brochure that had a picture of a swimming pool and happy seniors raising cocktails high in the air. "Funny, I don't remember seeing a swimming pool." I frowned.

"This looks like false advertisement to me. Maybe this Bridgett is running a scam," El added.

"I tried telling her that, but I had a lawyer look over the lease and he said there was no way I could get out of it without forfeiting my deposit. That's too much money to lose for a man on a fixed income. My son put up the money for me."

"I'd have to agree with that. Do you happen to have a copy of the contract? My boyfriend, Andrew Hart, is a lawyer. I'd sure love for him to look over the lease."

He rolled over to the table and dug through a pile of mail. "Anything to get you two out of here. And I mean that in the nicest way," he said with sarcasm as he handed the lease to me.

I tucked the brochure under my arm. "Thanks, Jack."

I made for the door and he added, "Let me know if Andrew finds a loophole. I'd love to bail from this place. They don't even have any of the activities they advertised either."

"At least you're not stuck cleaning rooms." With that, we left and I turned to Ernie. "I guess that settles it. Your brother did walk toward the swamp."

"Maybe he was looking for the swimming pool," he laughed. "If you'll excuse me I have some business to take care of in town."

I led the way as I went back to our room and once the door closed I stated, "I just knew that Bridgett was up to no good. I'm positive she stole our money now."

Eleanor sunk into a chair. "He never said she was a thief."

"No, but maybe Sheriff Peterson did send the money for our deposit. She has some scheme going on here. First she collects the deposits and then refuses to let the residents get out of their leases."

"She's dirty all right," Dorothy sighed. "Taking advantage of seniors like that."

"Why didn't you tell us Dorothy?"

She wrung her hands. "I didn't know. Frank handles all of the financial transactions. All I knew was that we were going to Florida."

"And Frank didn't question anything when we got here?"

"No. Bridgett was so insistent that we work here. I don't think we even thought about going back home." She sighed. "I miss Frank terribly. Can't we go downstairs and find him? If that Eunice woman has her hooks in Frank already ... I'll claw out her eyes!"

El rubbed both arms like she remembered all too well the clawing she endured by Dorothy. "Don't do that, but we'll help you out. I'll box the woman in the nose. I could cozy up to Frank and turn the tables on him."

"Like how?"

"We could get into a fight and I could act like I hurt you real bad."

"I bet Frank would spring into action then," I said in enthusiasm. "It will be just like a cage match."

Dorothy smiled. "Thank you, girls. I'd be lost without you here."

I patted Dorothy's arm. "Don't worry. This is bound to work."

Chapter Sixteen

I dressed in jeans and a yellow sleeveless blouse. Who knew how tonight's activities would go? I might as well don my battle gear. I slipped my swollen feet into a pair of sneakers, mindful to be sure to loosen the laces.

El pounced into the room like a puma. She adjusted the girls up a tad and asked, "How do I look?"

I examined her scoop neck pink top and leggings, stifling a laugh. "Well, that's certainly a show stopper." I stared at her high cleavage. "How did you manage to get your breasts to look so perky?"

Hands flew to her hips. "Whatever do you mean?"

"That you're too top heavy for it to be a natural process. You forget I have been your friend a long time."

"I rolled up a few socks and put them in the bottom of my bra."

I expected as much. "A few, or like a dozen."

"No need to be nasty. I just hope this works." El turned at Dorothy's approach.

Dorothy pulled down her white skirt, smoothing her paisley button up blouse into place. "D-Do I look okay?"

El closed the space between them and unbuttoned a few more buttons. "There, that's better."

Dorothy gasped. "Eleanor, do you want my breasts popping out?"

"Yes," I agreed with Dorothy. "We can't be having a wardrobe malfunction."

"Dorothy has a nice rack. She should show it off more."

"If she does that, half of the men in the room will be trying to paw at her."

"Well, the girl that did my mammogram said my breasts look good for a woman my age," Dorothy gushed. "I just have always dressed conservatively."

El applied red lipstick to Dorothy's lips. "You need to change your thought pattern if you want Frank back."

"Do you really think so? But I doubt Frank is interested in that sort of thing. We aren't even intimate anymore."

"That's silly," I said thinking about Andrew. "Life isn't over just because you're over seventy, dear."

Eleanor took out a blush brush and applied a fair amount to her cheeks. "It's an important thing to men. Frank might be old, but he's not dead. Why else do you think he has been checking me out all these years?"

"Because you're a floozy and not afraid to show your wares."

El shook her head at Dorothy, obviously letting the floozy comment drop. "What can I say, I like attention."

I smirked. "The wrong kind, usually."

"Well, it caught me Mr. Wilson."

I'd rather not visualize Eleanor with Mr. Wilson. "Oh, and here I thought he caught you with his tuna casserole."

She chuckled. "He does make a mean casserole."

I glided to the patio and looked out toward the

swamp. Apparently the sheriff hadn't made good on his promise to search the swamp if Bragsworth didn't turn up. Birds screeched and frogs chirped, but so far no screams. At this point I wondered what a missing pilot, a jewelry thief, the disappearances of two maids, and now a missing resident had in common. Then there were the boys at Homeland Security. What's their angle? What packet were they looking for? They never searched us back at the airport, so why show up with a search warrant? What Bridgett was doing thus far wasn't illegal, although dead wrong. I'll have to bring Andrew in on this.

Eleanor answered a sharp knock at the door. Andrew strolled into the room with a whistle. "Wow, what are you ladies up to tonight?"

I went to the dresser and retrieved the brochure and lease contract. "We're helping Dorothy get Frank back."

His eyes searched mine. "And how, may I ask?"

"Eleanor is going to come on to Frank. Then Dorothy is going to get into a fight with her. Maybe if Frank sees Dorothy hurt, he'll come to her rescue."

Eleanor chuckled when Andrew gave her a sharp look. "I'm not going to really hurt her. We'll play it off like it's for real is all."

Dorothy swiped a hand over her brow. "I'm glad to hear that. I'd hate to hurt you, Eleanor."

"You girls have been fighting for years. It would be completely believable that El would try and steal Frank away and a fight would ensue," I said with a nod.

Andrew patted Dorothy's arm. "You better hurry. I tried to keep Frank from Eunice, but she's latched onto him."

"I told you so. It's hopeless," Dorothy cried.

El pulled open the door. "It's show time. Give me a ten minute head start and then come down, Dorothy. Okay?" The door closed behind her and Dorothy sat on the cream couch, fidgeting with a grey curl near her ear.

Andrew's eyes widened as I handed him the papers. "Frank Winston gave me his lease and this brochure. I was hoping you could look them over."

"Why is that important?"

"The brochure is a complete falsehood. There's no swimming pool or activities as advertised and there's a twenty-five thousand dollar deposit that would be forfeited if the resident leaves before the end of winter. I believe Sheriff Clem Peterson back home sent the deposit with the pilot."

"You mean your stolen packet from your purse?"

"Exactly. It seems to me that Bridgett is running some kind of scam on these seniors."

"I'll look over the contract, but please be careful. I'd hate to have something bad happen to you." He kissed me just then and I nearly swooned. How was it possible for me to still feel butterflies when I was near this man?

I left the room with Dorothy, giving Andrew plenty of time to go over the contract. We strolled into the commons room with an agitated Eleanor standing near a pool table. When my eyes met hers I felt like I swallowed a stone. Eunice and Frank were at the card table playing cards and she was nearly in his lap! I rushed to Eleanor who gripped my arm, digging her fingernails into it. "It's worse than I thought. Maybe we're too late."

"No way. I can't let Dorothy down, but how am I going to get in-between those two?"

I shook my head and held Dorothy back before she let loose on Eunice. "That bitch!" Dorothy spewed in my ear.

Eleanor rounded the table and squeezed herself between Eunice and Frank. "What's cookin'? El asked Frank. She stared at the cards he held. "Fold, Frank, that's an awful hand."

Frank threw the cards up. "Thanks, Eleanor. You could have at least whispered." His eyes bulged slightly as he looked at Eleanor's ample bosom. "I missed you, toots. Where have you been?"

"I've been looking for Eunice's husband, Eugene. It seems she has forgotten all about him already." She hooked her arm through Frank's. "I thought you and I could go outside and gaze at the stars."

Dorothy rubbed her knuckles. "I'll show that Eleanor some stars," she hissed.

I grabbed Dorothy's hand and pulled her behind a large plant. "It's all part of the plan, remember?"

Frank chuckled. "Why, that's a good idea, Eleanor."

Eunice's lips tightened. "Go find yourself your own man. This one is mine."

"Butt out before I head butt you," El exclaimed. "Me and Frank go way back. Isn't that right, Frank?"

"It sure is, but I kinda like you both. I hope I don't have to choose just one of you. I'll be filing for divorce soon and I don't want to tie myself down to just one woman."

I wanted to clobber Frank about now. How could he

do this to Dorothy?

"Go away, Eunice, before I lose my temper. I've waited too long to be with Frank as it is."

"What's going on?" an angry Mr. Wilson asked. "Peaches, you said you'd be true."

Oh, great, what timing. Not only did we now have a Casanova, but we had an irate frail Mr. Wilson ready to do battle. He was going to mess the whole plan up.

As Mr. Wilson swung his walker, Eleanor scattered away and it caught Frank just under the chin. Boom! Frank hit the floor, rattling the poker chips. I couldn't stop Dorothy now. She elbowed her way to Frank's side. "Oh, Frank. Are you okay?"

Frank raised his head. "Go away, Dorothy. I told you b-before that I-I wanted a divorce."

"No, Frank. I won't leave you and I won't let you divorce me either. These women will have to kill me before I let them have you. I love you honey," Dorothy cried.

Frank tried to stand, but fell back down.

"You dumb ass," she spouted at Mr. Wilson. "Are you trying to kill him? He barely hears as it is."

"I've never noticed," Eunice said. "He's responded to every word I've said. Maybe he's just selective who he listens to."

Dorothy took on a ninja pose and kicked Eunice. Boom again! She hit the ground next to Frank, but she didn't stay there. She jumped back up and swung her purse at Dorothy, catching her alongside her ear. Dorothy hissed like a cobra. "You bitch!" They circled, trying to get at each other, but Eleanor got between them and put a hand on each of their heads.

"Ladies, stop before one of you breaks something!" Eleanor shouted. Losing her grip on them, they both tumbled to the floor with a thump. Claws were raised and hair was pulled, but neither of them stopped.

I ran forward. "Do something, Frank!"

"Are you plain loco? Dorothy obviously has never hit you before."

"She's your wife."

"And your point is?"

"Eunice is hurting her. What's the matter with you? Move. Do something."

"Stop it, Dorothy. If I had known you'd get like this, I'd never have thrown you out. This is rather exciting."

When I followed Frank's line of vision I saw that Dorothy's bosom was exposed. I yanked a tablecloth off a nearby table causing dishes to crash to the floor. I threw it to Dorothy who covered herself the best she could. Frank then helped Dorothy to her feet. Eunice's eyes glazed over and she scrambled up and grabbed a decanter of wine intent on hitting Dorothy with it, but she was whirled around by Eleanor who then head butted her. Eunice slumped to the floor and I emitted a long sigh. It's over finally.

"Oh, Dorothy. I was just trying to make you jealous. How could I ever replace you?"

How indeed, I thought.

Frank rubbed his bald head. "You really got in some good licks. Some nerve, that woman … accusing me of killing her husband one minute and all over me the next."

"And what about Eleanor?"

"Somehow I think you put her up to this." He handed Mr. Wilson his walker. "Sorry, old man. You know I'd never steal Eleanor from you. Any woman who eats your tuna casserole on a regular basis is a keeper."

Mr. Wilson squeaked his walker toward Eleanor. "I sure love your attire. Maybe we should retire to my room," he whistled. "I love you, Peaches."

El gave Wilson a bear hug. "I love you too, you old dog. It was so exciting to see you stand up for what's yours – me!"

I was stuck standing there watching both couples swap spit. It made me wish Andrew was here now. So the plan worked out, but not exactly like I had planned. I searched the crowd of seniors filing into the room and noticed Eunice was long gone. Maybe she was off licking her wounds.

I was just glad Dorothy and Frank made up. It's hard to see those two fighting. They are more made for each other than any other couple I have ever known. So what if he turned his hearing aid down sometimes. If it kept them together, it was worth it.

Bridget glided into the room with a frown and righted chairs without a word until she blared, "I swear in all my days, I have never met such a rowdy group of seniors before."

I smiled to myself. She sure got that one right. I should warn her that it would only get more interesting. What can I say; we Michigan folks know how to shake it up.

I left the room hoping El would really spend the night with Mr. Wilson, giving Andrew and I time together. Andrew grimaced when I entered my room. He had the couch spread out with papers. "Boy, that sure is an extensive looking lease contract." He raised a brow. "And from what I can see, an airtight one."

I picked up the brochure. "So you couldn't find a loophole either?"

"Either?"

"Well, Jack did mention he had a lawyer look over the agreement too and he said the same thing as you." I pursed my lips. "Could we get Bridgett with false advertisement?"

"Did you sign a contract, Aggie?"

"No. Sheriff Peterson did, but he seemed to make a separate deal with Bridgett. We're supposed to be cleaning rooms for our room and board."

"Did he give Bridgett a deposit?"

"I'm not sure. I found a packet with money in the amount of twenty-five thousand, but that's about it."

"The stolen money?"

"Yes, and Bridgett hasn't pressed you to pay her any deposit."

"Not so far."

Andrew stretched, revealing his tight abs. "She's guilty of fraud. You can't advertise things that simply don't exist."

"The swimming pool is a biggie for me. That, and the omission of a swamp out back." I fanned myself with the brochure. "It sure is hot in here."

Andrew took his shirt off. "It is now." With that we retired to the bedroom.

Chapter Seventeen

I sat on the bed, pulling on purple crop pants and a white blouse. Grabbing my foot, I crossed it over the other, the only way I'd ever get my ballerina style flats on. The older I get the harder it is to do even the simplest of tasks. Andrew had left first thing in the morning, promising to be back by dinner. That left me plenty of time to go downtown and visit Julie at Julie's Jewels. I had to find out if that ski mask was the same one used in the robberies.

I listened to the shower running. Eleanor had crept in the door an hour ago. I'm sure she thought I'd be mad that she had baled on me last night, but nothing could be further from the truth. I was just glad that Andrew was here. Eleanor needed to spend sometime with Mr. Wilson. He was her beau, after all.

The water cut off and Eleanor surfaced five minutes later with a towel partially covering her body. She skipped to the bedroom and dressed in silence. Eleanor's beet red face even looked more so with the red shirt she wore. She also wore matching red shorts that showed only fair skin.

"I know, right?" Eleanor said as she winced. "It hurts horribly."

"How did you manage to only burn your face and arms?"

She shrugged. "I guess it was the magnification of

the ocean. I should have listened to you, but I swear I wore sunscreen."

"You just are cursed with fair skin, is all." I handed her a container with white lotion. "Here, put this on."

Eleanor slathered on the lotion, wincing. "What's the plan for today?"

"We're going to Julie's Jewels today. I want to question her about that ski mask."

"Sounds good. I'm ready." With that we left the room, running into Martha in the hallway.

"Hello, Mom. I'll do the cleaning today. Bridgett said otherwise we had to come up with twenty-five thousand dollars for a deposit. What on earth is she talking about?"

"That's what all the residents pay."

"Do you have that kind of dough?"

"Nope. Thanks for doing the cleaning. Eleanor and I are going into town to sleuth."

Martha pushed her cart down the hallway. "Don't get into any trouble."

We found Darcy in the kitchen barking orders to Mr. Wilson and Frank Alton, who had a smile plastered to his face."

I waved at Frank. "Hello, Frank."

"It's a great day to be alive!" he shouted.

I pulled Darcy aside. "Can we borrow your car again? I promise we'll be back before dinner."

"Be my guest," she said as she handed me the keys.

Eleanor and I made for the door and luckily didn't run into Bridgett. I'd hate to try and explain where we were going. Once we settled ourselves into the car I tore out of the drive and soon was driving along Ocean

View Avenue. The waves were high today and so was the wind. Sailboats bobbed in the distance with yachts further out.

I parked on the main drag not far from where Eleanor and I were shot at not long ago, which made me more than a little nervous. Hopefully we wouldn't run into the man with the hawk-like nose.

When we arrived at Julie's Jewels, cameras were positioned, one on each corner of the room with a round bubble containing yet another camera in the middle of the room, which panned from right to left.

Julie was behind the counter spraying glass cleaner on the display cases. Today her dark hair was curled and she wore a blue, lightweight chiffon dress.

"Hello again," she greeted us.

Indicating the cameras, I remarked, "I see you have made the necessary adjustments."

"Yes, and so far my business has picked up, but I have to be honest. Every time the doorbell rings my heart jumps into my throat."

"I don't blame you, but the cameras should give you some security." I frowned. "I hope I'm not pestering you, but I was wondering if Sheriff Peterson brought a ski mask over."

She pressed her lips into a line. "I was told to keep that quiet. How did you hear about it?"

"We were there when the ski mask was found."

"I see. Well, like I told the sheriff it looks like that mask, but I'm not certain it was the same one worn by the robber. I don't have any experience in these matters. We don't see many masks here in Florida."

I examined my face in the glass of the case. "I bet

not. Did he mention who might have worn the mask?"

"Yes, Eugene Bragsworth, but he hardly seems the type. He used to date my mom and he sure seems like a nice enough man. I also heard he's now missing."

"When was he dating your mom?"

"About a few weeks ago."

My mouth slacked open. "That's strange, because we were told he was married."

"Oh, my!"

"He's missing all right, but his twin brother is in town."

"Twin?"

"Did your mother mention if Bragsworth was a twin?"

"Well, no, but maybe you should talk to my mother about that. She's in the back."

I tapped my fingers on the counter as Julie went in search of her mother, bringing her back.

"I'm Priscilla. I believe you were asking about me."

Eleanor stepped forward. "Yes, I was wondering about Eugene Bragsworth."

She fluffed her curly red hair. "Well, we only dated a few weeks. It's nothing to make much of."

"Two weeks can be a long time, dear," I said. "Did he mention his family at all?"

"No. Like I said—"

"Or wife," Eleanor interjected.

She came unglued. "Wife! Why no! He's not married, is he?"

"It appears that he is," I gently informed her. "Her name is Eunice."

She pulled out a tissue from her pocket with a shaky

hand. "Oh, my. I swear I didn't know."

I patted Pricilla's hand. "I'm sorry, dear. I'm sorry we mentioned it. I was just wondering about his family, is all."

"He seemed so nice and then suddenly he quit calling."

"I know the type," Eleanor said. "And you're better off without him."

Julie stroked her chin in thought. "I wonder how many other women he dated in town?"

"Beats me, but if that Bragsworth was the jewelry thief, you can at least rest easier."

Julie smiled sympathetically at her mother. "I really had hopes that he was one of the good ones. Ever since my father passed, my mother hasn't been herself."

"Poor dear. I'm a widow, too, and I know how hard it is to get back into the dating game, but it can be done. Have faith."

We bid the ladies goodbye and sauntered out of the store, buying a hotdog with the last of my bra money. I wondered if Sheriff Peterson had any leads about our purses. We walked into a candy store and I asked the girl at the counter if I could use the phone.

"Who are you calling, Agnes?"

"Sheriff Peterson." Ignoring El I spoke to the person who answered the phone. "Is Sheriff Peterson there? I filed a report about a missing purse and I was wondering." I listened intently to the woman on the other end. "Oh, I see. Thanks."

"What gives?"

"It seems that Peterson is out at Sunny Brooke. I wonder if he's conducting a search?"

"I don't know, Agnes, but we should high-tail it there to find out."

I blinked a few times as I spotted the man with the hawk-like nose leaning against a newspaper rack.

I gripped El's arm in a death-like grip. When El winced, she gazed across the room and gasped. We slowly backed up and ran out the door. Loud footsteps trailed behind us as we stumbled onto another street.

"Why do you two keep running from me?"

I whirled. "Why are you following us?"

El and I stood both shaking like a leaf. "Yeah, buzz off," Eleanor said. "We're taken."

He reached into his shirt pocket and I yanked El into a nearby store. We meandered through the sporting goods store with Mr. Hawk Nose in hot pursuit. El pulled down a net that held basketballs and they bounced along behind us.

"Yelp!" Mr. Hawk Nose cried as he tumbled, landing in a heap on the floor, but we kept going. That was until Eleanor spied pink revolvers in a case. "Hey, we need one of these." I grabbed El's arm and dug my nails into her. "Move!"

We managed to leave the store through a back door that opened up into a bikini shop, but we didn't stop until we were on the beach, and only then did we take a breath. "I can't move anymore," El admitted. "I'm exhausted."

I tried to speak but couldn't. I had to catch my breath. "We need a gun," I finally said.

"Did I hear you correctly?" a female near us asked. Her dark hair was pulled back into a ponytail and it bounced as she glanced to and fro, presumably to make sure nobody was within earshot.

"Yes, but we don't have any identification or time to wait for the waiting period," I informed her.

"Somebody is following us," El said. "He wants to off us."

"I see. Well, my father is here in town for the gun show. Do you have any money?"

El reached into her bra and flashed the cash. "I only have a hundred."

"Eleanor, that's the last of our cash."

"I know, but dang it. We need a gun."

"You two remind me of my grandmother and her friend. I'll help you out."

We followed the girl to a car parked in an alley. She lifted the trunk and it was loaded with guns!

"Oh my, a-are these legal? I'd hate to buy a gun that could kick us in the crotch later."

She frowned, but came up with a pink gun with a long barrel. "This one is legal. It's one of my grand-mother's favorites, but she upsized."

She placed it into my hands and I shook my head. "I don't know. It's awful big and we have no purse to put it in. Ours were stolen."

"I see. Not a problem."

She pulled out a large black handbag and handed it to me, but Eleanor intercepted it. "I'll be the one handling the pistol so I might as well carry the bag."

"Well, you are the bag lady, so okay."

Eleanor frowned and opened the bag waiting for the pistol to be placed inside, but the woman hesitated. Her eyes locked with mine. "Is it okay?"

With a swipe of my hand I answered, "Sure, she's

pretty good with a pistol."

"We both are, Aggie. She once had to kill an intruder."

"How awful. What is this country coming to?"

"We're from Michigan. We like to shoot stuff," Eleanor said, waiting for the gun to be placed inside. "I hope you can spare some bullets, too."

The girl put the gun into the bag and tossed in ammunition. "It's a .22, but that's more than enough to put a stop to any perp."

"Thanks. We have the Charter Arms Pink Ladies back home."

"This gun is way more accurate on account of the longer barrel. You won't be disappointed," the girl added. She then slammed the trunk closed and hopped in the car, backing it out of the alley while we made our way back toward the beach.

"She sure seemed nice," El said. "I wonder if we lost Mr. Hawk Nose."

"I'm not sure, but we better get back to Sunny Brooke before we spot him again. We can't very well pull a revolver out on a public beach."

"True, Aggie. We need to find out why Sheriff Peterson is out at Sunny Brooke before he leaves. Maybe he'll be more forthcoming today."

We carefully made our way to the car and hopped in, zooming back to Sunny Brooke. When we arrived, Sheriff Peterson was on the front porch with Andrew. I pulled into a parking spot and we walked toward the men.

With a raised brow, Andrew asked, "Where have you been, Aggie?"

Looking at the purse El held, I answered. "Purse shopping. It seems I have run out of cash to purchase my own."

Andrew placed a hand on his wallet. "I'd be more than happy to spot you two a loan until you get more cash."

Peterson's lips curved into a smile. "Good news. We found your missing purses."

I sighed in relief. "Where?"

"In town. A good Samaritan turned them in. Your ID is still inside."

My heart leapt at that tidbit of information. "Great! Where are they?"

"Inside. I left them with Bridgett."

I ran toward the door. "You what?"

When I reached the front counter Bridgett handed us our purses. "I wonder how your purses got into town."

"Indeed. Maybe *somebody* got a little scared and ditched them."

"That must be it. I'm so happy that your purses were found. Is everything still in the bag?"

I clutched my purse to my chest. "It had better be."

"Check," Peterson said as he entered. "We need to know if anything is missing."

I sat on a cream chair and rummaged through my purse, yanking out the contents as my heart leapt into my throat. "It's gone."

"What's missing?" Andrew asked.

Tears dotted my eyes. "Oh, nothing. Just a packet containing twenty-five thousand in cash."

"It was in an envelope," Eleanor said. "Agnes found

it on the airplane after the pilot was killed."

"Where did you get that kind of cash?" Bridgett asked, her eyes narrowing.

"I think Sheriff Clem Peterson gave the pilot the money for our deposit presumably."

Bridgett's face paled. "Deposit?"

"Yes. It's part of the deal for staying here, isn't it?"

El gripped her handbag tightly. "Yes, the residents pay you twenty-five Gs and you hold it over their heads."

Bridgett grabbed at the neck of her blouse as if feeling cornered. "I'm not sure what you heard."

"We happen to know that you make the residents sign the lease and wire you the money before they realize what it's *really like here*."

She darted a glance toward the sheriff. "I'm not sure what they're talking about."

"Is the swamp in the brochure?"

El crossed her arms. "And I don't see any swimming pool here either or any of the activities mentioned in the brochure."

"That's an old brochure. We're printing new ones."

"I bet. You're running a scam here. If the residents leave after they get here, you pocket the twenty-five thousand dollar deposit."

Bridgett eyed Sheriff Peterson. "It's a perfectly legal lease. Many other communities have the same contract."

"Where did my brother come up with that kind of money? Sheriffs don't make that kind of money."

I glanced at Peterson. "How would I know?"

"Well, did you clarify this with my brother or are

you just guessing here?"

"It has to be him. I saw him hand the pilot a packet, and when the pilot was killed, I found it on the airplane. Maybe it was a robbery attempt."

"Yeah," El started. "Maybe they were planning to off us all and take the money."

Peterson scratched his head. "You're way out there now. Twenty-five thousand isn't enough to justify killing a bunch of old folks."

"Who you calling old?" El spat. "And people have been offed for far less."

"True," I agreed.

Peterson yanked his trousers up. "Homeland Security called me and told me that the pilot wasn't found dead or alive. So what makes you think he was killed, Agnes?"

"Because we saw him go down."

"The man with the hawk-like nose killed him," El cut in. "He's following us."

Andrew's face reddened. "Where? How?"

I rubbed Andrew's arm. "We saw him twice in town."

"He chased us today," El added.

"I knew I shouldn't have let you two out of my sight," Andrew spat. "Did he threaten you?"

"No!"

"I'm calling my brother," Peterson said.

When I looked up, Bridgett was missing. How had she slipped away unnoticed?

"She's gone," I told El.

El whirled around. "We found her out. She might be high-tailing it with our money."

Peterson tried to console us after he powered off his cell phone. “My brother said he only gave the pilot the directions to Turtle Dune Beach.”

I frowned. “So where did the twenty-five Gs come from?”

“I don’t know but we need to find that man with the hawk nose before this gets out of hand. We’ll need you two to do a composite sketch.”

“It seems Bridgett snuck off. She has to be the one who stole the money,” I informed the sheriff. “She probably dropped our purses off in town to throw us off the trail. She’s the one that would have had access to the lockers.”

“I’m with you on that one, Agnes.” Peterson radioed in for more deputies.

Chapter Eighteen

Within ten minutes the place was crawling with cops. In the commons room, Mr. Wilson was playing cards with Frank and Dorothy Alton. "Have you seen Bridgett?" I asked the startled group.

"She ran through here," Mr. Wilson croaked out as he tossed poker chips on the table.

We moved on to the next room, which was the dining room, but the only thing in that room was rows of white clothed tables. "Maybe we should try the kitchen," I suggested.

Peterson led the way and shouldered open the door. Darcy stood there looking guilty with a cupcake in her hand as she faced down the deputies. "You caught me. I swear I never meant to steal the cupcake, but it's a new flavor and I wanted to make sure it tasted good."

"What flavor is it?" El asked in amusement.

"Raspberry swirl with lime frosting."

"That sounds interesting."

"El, please."

"Sorry. I'm hungry."

"Did Bridgett duck in here?"

"Why, no, but there sure was a commotion out back. Is that why all the cops are here?"

"Not exactly."

"Oh, and here I had hoped they would have been tearing up the swamp looking for Mr. Bragsworth."

"Eugene or Ernie?"

She laughed. "You're funny, Agnes."

We left the kitchen and followed a hallway that opened up onto the patio area where picnic tables were lined up on a concrete slab. There was also a screen patio door that stood wide open!

"Maybe you ladies should stay here," Peterson suggested. "I'd hate to see either of you hurt."

"So finally you're taking this seriously?"

"I wish you had mentioned earlier about the money and the lease agreement."

"I only recently learned of the agreement and I really thought your brother had sent the money."

"Why on earth would he send that kind of money via a pilot? He would have wired the money."

"True, but one just never knows what your brother might do."

"You should give him a little credit. He's a great sheriff."

I grabbed at my throat. "No doubt from our help."

He laughed. "You two haven't helped solve that many crimes. My brother has a great record. He always gets his man eventually."

It was the eventually that had me worried, but maybe he was right. I should give ole Peterson back home some credit. If I hadn't known better, I'd have thought he sent us here to solve the disappearances of the maids, but thus far, we had come up empty. We did happen to lose twenty-five Gs, though. If only I had kept that money on my person and not in that dang locker, maybe then things wouldn't have gone so south.

"So what's next?"

"I plan on bringing Bridgett in for questioning. The disappearance of that kind of money is pretty significant." He frowned. "I'll have to bring Homeland Security in on this too, as they were asking about a packet that was left on the airplane. Putner and Palmer I think their names were."

I gulped. That's all I needed, to be questioned again by those two. Now, what would money and Homeland Security have in common? And what about the pilot? Where was he? Tomorrow first thing I'm heading back to the airport to look for clues. That is if Sheriff Peterson would give us the directions. Maybe he could take us there.

"What about the maintenance man, Jamie Odell? We haven't questioned him yet."

"Good point. I don't see Bridgett out here. Let's find Jamie."

Peterson barked out orders for the deputies to search the perimeter of the property, and we made way for the front counter where Jessica Bolf stood with limbs trembling. She had a finger wound around one of the long curls of her hair and the other was toying with the button of her burgundy blouse. When none of us said a word, she looked puzzled. "What?" she asked. "How would I know where Miss Bridgett went off to? It's so unlike her to dart off like that. Maybe she's in the restroom."

"I don't remember asking you anything yet, dear," I said.

"Oh," she gasped. "I just don't know where she could be, is all."

"You said as much, but where is the maintenance

man, Jamie Odell?"

"I don't know, but I can call him."

Obviously she didn't know much of anything.

She pulled a phone out and called Jamie to the front desk via a two way. We waited, watching as Jessica shuffled nervously under our stares. Her face lit up when Jamie walked forward. He was a tall, thin man who wore gray Dockers pants and shirt, his dark hair slicked back like the Fonz. When he glanced at the sheriff, he expelled a breath. "Can I help you?"

"Why, yes," the sheriff motioned to El and me. "I'm looking into the theft of the ladies' purses a few days ago. Did you take them out of the lockers?"

He pointed at his chest. "Me? No. Miss Bridgett would have my ass if I ever touched anyone's belongings. She has always been very clear about that."

"Did you see anyone behind the counter who didn't belong there?"

"No, sir. I don't even go back there unless Jessica or Bridgett is there."

I took over the questioning. "So according to you, you have never taken anything out of the locker area."

"Not unless I was asked to cut a lock off a locker."

"And have you cut any locks off recently."

"Nope. Miss Bridgett keeps the extra keys up here so there is no need to."

"So cutting off locks is to a minimum now?"

"Exactly. Our residents are very trustworthy around here."

"Thanks for the information, Jamie," I said. I then turned toward the sheriff with a questionable look.

"Thanks, Jamie. If you happen to see Bridgett

please let her know we're looking for her," Peterson said. "Please go back to your room, Agnes. I'll let you know if Bridgett surfaces."

"Wh-What? Why can't we take part in the search?"

"I appreciate your help, but there is no sense in you two waiting around for nothing."

Andrew walked forward with two take-out containers. "Here's lunch."

I frowned. "Let me guess, tuna casserole."

"Yes, it's all Mr. Wilson wants to make. I guess nobody told him everyone is sick of it."

Eleanor slapped her leg laughing. "Oh, they told him all right. He just can't help himself."

We took the food back to my room and settled back on the couch until I noticed the deputies outside. "Apparently Peterson is doing a thorough search this time."

"Yeah," El agreed. "I'd have thought they would have searched the swamp for Eugene Bragsworth by now. I wonder why they haven't yet."

"I wonder that, too, but maybe they are waiting the basic twenty-four hours first." I pursed my lips. "We need to find that pilot tomorrow."

Andrew raised a brow. "How are you planning to do that?"

"I was hoping Peterson could direct us to the airport where we first landed."

El's eyes crossed. "You mean the one where the pilot was offed?"

"We don't know for sure he's dead, but something definitely is wrong with this whole situation. First the pilot is supposedly shot, and then Putner and Palmer all but deny it even happened."

"Yes, and what would they want with a packet of money?"

"Then there is the whole deal with the missing persons. Is it connected to the missing money or jewelry thief?" El pulled out a fork. "What if the jewelry thief is right here and he stole the money?"

"But Bragsworth—"

"What if it's not Bragsworth at all, Aggie? We don't know for sure he was our guy."

"There was a ski mask in his room," I insisted.

Andrew rubbed my back. "Have you thought that perhaps it was planted? He is missing."

"That's true, but who else do we have to suspect? El and I saw the thief firsthand."

"Did he look like Bragsworth?"

"I don't know, but he was tall like the robber."

"Plenty of tall men around here if you ask me, Aggie," Eleanor pointed out.

"I'm drawing a blank here. Bridgett had access to the lockers is all I know, unless everyone is lying and that's a stretch."

Andrew stopped rubbing my back and poured himself a glass of wine. "You have yourself one humdinger of a case this time around, but at least nobody has turned up dead yet."

"Don't say that, Andrew. It's bad luck."

El shuddered. "I could forgo the discovery of a body this time around. I hate finding corpses."

"True El, but it's not like we have a choice. We don't find them on purpose."

"No," she chuckled. "They just happen to show up when we least expect it."

There was a knock at the door and Peterson was standing there when I squeaked it open. "Did you find Bridgett?"

"No, but we're sweeping the swamp. If she went in there, we'll find her. Unless you can think of another place she'd hole up."

"I don't know the woman well enough. Are you looking for Eugene Bragsworth while you're out there?"

"Yes, but we're only going to be able to do so much. It's too dangerous to be out in the swamp too long, what with the gators and snakes and all, but we'll do our best." With a nod he left.

"Well," I mumbled when the door closed. "At least they're searching the swamp."

Andrew sipped his wine. "Don't expect too much, Agnes. I imagine most of the swamp is impenetrable."

I frowned. That would figure. So much for me going into the swamp myself. I had hoped at least some of it was dry land, but here Andrew was dashing my hopes.

Where was Bridgett? There were only so many places somebody could hide in the retirement village… or so I thought.

"Let's check for Bridgett again," I suggested.

"I'm pooped, Aggie. Didn't you hear a word the sheriff said? They are searching the swamp and I suspect doing a good job looking for Bridgett. All we would do is get in the way."

"I can't believe you, El. We're senior snoops and no matter what, we're the ones who find the clues, not the sheriff."

El slapped her legs with her hands. "Not this time. Let the sheriff do his job."

I sat back in a huff. What happened to El? Had the heat sucked up her brain? I have never sat idly by while law enforcement did their job. Never! There had to be some way to find Bridgett. So far all the clues pointed to her. She's the one holding the deposits over the residents' heads. Maybe she wants to entice them to leave so she can pocket the money and just maybe that's why she stole our money. She might think she has a right to it seeing as how Peterson never paid a deposit for us. She's a crook.

"What's going on inside that head of yours, Agnes?" Andrew asked. "You're plotting. I know it."

"No, I just hope they find Bridgett, is all. Her hasty departure has to mean something. Why else would she just take off like that? She knows we're closing in on her and there isn't much room for escape. I'm glad the sheriff is finally in our court."

"I sure hope things work out the way you want Agnes, but you should know by now the odds are against you. It's just how your cases go. It wasn't long ago you suspected me of wrong doing."

"That was on our last case Andrew, and for the record, I just didn't like how you kept things from me."

He frowned. "I think you are way more secretive than me. Weren't you just at a stripper show not long ago?"

"Don't act so innocent. I know how you men are."

He threw up his hands. "Here we go again. Do I need to kiss you to stop you from putting your foot in your mouth?"

My mouth gaped open, but I then shut it, nearly losing my uppers.

"I love you, Agnes, even though Eleanor and you constantly put yourselves in danger. Did you bring your pink lady pistols to Florida with you?"

"Of course not. I anticipated passing through larger airports. I'd hate to be arrested!"

"You certainly have experience behind bars. You two are a couple of jail birds."

"We sure flew the coop fast that time," Eleanor said with a sly smile. "At least this Sheriff Peterson is more laid back."

I kept quiet about the pistol. I mean, how would I explain buying a gun from somebody's trunk no less? I was still shocked about that one. Hopefully we wouldn't have to use the gun. I exchanged a knowing glance with Eleanor who clammed up on mention of a gun, thankfully.

Andrew glanced at his watch and told us he'd catch up with us later. Once he was out the door I rambled on. "Thanks for not telling Andrew about the pistol we bought."

"He doesn't need to know everything. Besides, we don't even know if the gun will work or not, but I do feel confident having it." Eleanor transferred the pistol from the purse supplied by the girl who sold us the gun, to her black Gucci bag.

I clicked on the television and they were blabbering on about Secret Service. They were warning business to be on the lookout for counterfeit hundred dollar bills. There was an ongoing investigation in the state of Florida. My mind started to twist, but before I could say a word, Eleanor said, "Agnes, is there any way the money you had was counterfeit?"

"There is no way this has anything to do with the missing money. I'm sure the money I saw was real."

"How can you be positive?"

"I can't, but it can't look that much like real money."

"Did you look for a watermark? Only real money has them."

My head began to pound. "If it's counterfeit, the person who stole it wouldn't know unless...."

"They get caught with it," El added. "What a shock that would be to them," she snickered.

"Unless they don't get caught. Most counterfeiters pass a large amount of bills before they are found out."

"True, but with them spreading the word, they'd be caught for sure."

"We're getting off track here. There's no way the money wasn't real. It would be too much of a coincidence."

"Then why else would Putner and Palmer be asking about a packet from the airplane? It has to be it."

"You're doing quite a bit of guessing here, El. Unless somebody is busted, I won't believe it."

"Somebody connected to Sunny Brooke, you mean."

I massaged the back of my neck and walked to the patio, but I didn't see any deputies staked out. *The search couldn't have been over already*, I thought. *Surly the sheriff was still here.*

I called the front desk and Jessica confirmed that the sheriff and the rest of the cops had left. I hung up the phone irritated. "The sheriff left."

"I suppose the swamp was too much for them."

"That's bull, El. How can they give up on finding Bridgett so soon? We're going to have to find her ourselves."

She shrugged as she followed me out the door and into the dining room. We settled ourselves beside Mr. Wilson who sat next to Dorothy and Frank Alton who had their hands all over each other!

A smile split Mr. Wilson's face. "I keep telling them to get a room."

"Well, at least they made up."

"Easy for you to say. My room is next to theirs," Wilson complained.

I'd rather not have had that mental image in my brain. "Any sign of Bridgett?"

"Nope, but maybe she'll turn up since the fuzz left," Wilson mumbled. "They ruined our card game with all their traipsing around."

Frank smirked. "Aw, you're just mad I won all your money."

"No, I'm just mad they ruined my luck, is all."

"Cards are a game of chance, not luck. I don't believe in luck," I said as I interlaced my fingers on the table in front of me.

"Huh," Wilson spat. "Your whole sleuthing has been all luck. You're lucky to be alive." He slapped a hand on his leg laughing.

I stared down the gaunt Mr. Wilson with a raised brow. "I'll have you know that El and I have solved a variety of cases, including a cold case murder. We didn't do it by luck, I tell you."

"No, Agnes was given permission to go over the case files by Trooper Sales. She found out the handyman didn't do it."

"I guess not. He was murdered."

"Enough talk about the past. What I want to know is where Bridgett is."

Darcy sauntered out of the kitchen and served us cream of potato soup. "Eat up folks. I don't want to be here all night. Now way am I staying here after dark."

With a spoon halfway to my mouth I asked, "Why is that?"

"Because people are dropping off like flies and even the sheriff can't figure it out."

"Who's in charge if Bridgett doesn't show up?"

"It runs pretty smooth around here most of the time. All she ever did was get in the way. Our wages have been paid in advance."

"You were paid for the whole season in advance? What a strange idea."

She chuckled. "I suppose it was as an incentive to stay. After the maids disappeared, it made most of the hired help a little nervous. Plenty of us wanted to quit right then, but Bridgett paid us the advance if we promised to stay."

"If she was so desperate then why not press the sheriff to search the swamp? There has to be a logical reason the maids disappeared."

"Well," she rubbed her arms. "You saw how long that one lasted."

She waddled away and left us to our soup. She sure hit that one on the head. I wanted to ring that sheriff's neck. He couldn't have searched the swamp for more than a half hour.

The next course came and went and I pushed myself away from the table. "Well, El, I'm full. I suppose we should just turn in for the night."

El glanced toward Wilson. "Yes, but if you don't mind I'm going to stay with Wilson tonight."

Andrew entered the room with an exhausted Martha who all but collapsed into a chair. "Where have you been all day, Martha?"

"Cleaning rooms while you were gallivanting all over town. See if I help you out again. I should have just stayed at the beach."

Darcy came forward with food for Martha who turned her nose up at the fish and soup. "I'm a vegan. Don't you have any salad in that kitchen?"

"We do. Help yourself to it," Darcy said as she pulled off her apron. "I'm heading home for the night. See you folks tomorrow."

I stood and Andrew gave me a hug. "Are you coming back to the room soon, Martha?"

"And listen to you old folks go at it? No, thanks. I'll sleep on the couch in the lobby first."

"I hardly think that is safe. Give us a half hour and it'll be safe to come inside," I insisted. "I couldn't bear it if you went missing, too."

She nodded, shooing us off. Andrew and I made our way to the room with our hands all over each other. If it was good enough for the Altons, it was good enough for us. Love was certainly in the air.

Chapter Nineteen

In the morning, Andrew and I crept out, mindful not to awaken Martha who slept on the couch. That was until Eleanor trounced inside, slamming open the door and hitting the wall with a thump!

"Aargh! Can't you old folks keep it down?" Martha swung her legs off the couch and headed to the bedroom with pillow in hand.

Andrew slid open the screen door, walked out onto the patio and shielded his eyes as the morning sun was blinding. It was then that I heard a thumping noise. "Ba-boom ... ba-boom."

"What in the hell is that?"

I raced outside and stared toward the swamp. "No, not that." I stared at a shadow that moved in the wind on the floor of the patio. When I looked up I gasped, but I couldn't say anything until I finally choked out. "It's Bridgett!"

We raced up the stairs and stumbled into a room. And there on the balcony was Bridgett swaying in the wind, a tight rope around her neck.

"I-s is she d-dead?"

"From the grey appearance of her skin, I'd say yes," Andrew alleged.

Eleanor's eyes bulged, her whole body trembling. "How long has she been hanging up there?"

"Why are you asking me, El? I was with Andrew all

night."

"I meant has she been hiding in this room all night?"

I shrugged. "I'm not sure if this is even Bridgett's room at all." Looking around, all the furnishings were covered in thick plastic. "Maybe this is a spare room."

"Well," Eleanor began. "Obviously this was where she was hiding out. It's no wonder the sheriff couldn't find her."

"True, El." My limbs involuntarily shook. "I must admit that I'm a surprised to find Bridgett this way. I didn't see her as suicidal."

"Maybe her back was up against the wall and she was guilty of stealing the money in your purse."

I shook my head. "I just don't believe she took her own life."

Eleanor scoffed at that. "Well, she is hanging there. What else do you need to see to convince you? A suicide note?"

"Yes. That would do."

I picked up the phone and called 911 to report the finding of a body at Sunny Brooke.

I then examined the balcony. There was an overturned chair with skid marks that dug into the wooden floor. "It sure seems consistent with suicide, but Bridgett couldn't have thought she had no alternative. The sheriff had nothing on her for sure. He just wanted to question her."

Sheriff Peterson appeared at the door with a dark expression on his face. "Who found the body?"

"We did just now. My room is on the first floor and we heard an awful thumping. I had all but forgotten about Bridgett. We just got up," I informed him.

He examined the balcony floor and raised a brow. "It's consistent with a suicide. Did you find a note?"

"Why no, but I haven't looked for one either. How long were you searching the swamp?"

"Not long. It's pretty bad back there. I'd suggest staying away unless you want to die by snakebite."

I shuddered. "No, thanks." I glanced around, but didn't see any note. "She didn't leave a note behind if she committed suicide."

Peterson's brows furrowed. "What do you mean *if*?"

"Sure, she's dead by hanging, but only a coroner can determine if she died beforehand."

El nodded. "Aggie is right. She might have other injuries that suggest otherwise."

"Yes, like a head wound. Should we cut the body down at least?"

"Nope. We'll leave it for the forensic guys. I must say this is the first time I have hauled off a body from Sunny Brooke."

"Are you sure? It's a retirement village."

"Those were all natural causes. So far all I have been called here for is missing person cases."

"Three so far, right?"

He glanced about the room. "Yes, and I hope there won't be more."

"I just don't believe Bridgett would kill herself. There simply isn't enough evidence to suggest that."

"I have been a sheriff for years and you just never know. She was feeling cornered so she sought the only way out."

"Cornered from what, a few questions from the local sheriff? She could easily snow you like she had previously."

"Now, Agnes. I'm experienced and the coroner will rule this a suicide, I'm sure of it."

I visibly rolled my eyes. "We'll see."

"You won't now. Unless you have something more to add, I'd ask you all to leave and let us handle the investigation."

"Investigation? You sound like you have already made up your mind about the cause of death."

"Agnes, please."

I whirled. "Fine then, but my guess is that it will be a cover up."

He grabbed my arm and got in my face. "I don't like how you said that. It's not in my interest to cover anything up. Maybe with Bridgett gone, things will calm down."

I gasped. "You say that like you suspect Bridgett of more than the robbery of the money. Was she a person of interest in the recent disappearances?"

"Everyone is a suspect until I find out otherwise."

"And I suppose we're suspects in Bragsworth's disappearance?"

"Frank sure is, but yes. You all are suspects."

"You're just like your brother, Clem. I'm getting sick of being blamed just because someone turns up dead that I happen to suspect of a crime. What of the ski mask? I heard from Julie at Julie's Jewels that she identified the mask as that worn by the robber."

He adjusted the waistband of his trousers. "Who told you to be questioning her? That is official police business. I'm handling the investigation or did you forget?"

"No. I remember. You keep getting in the way. Did you do any DNA analysis of the ski mask, like was it even Bragsworth's?"

"Of course not. People can have a ski mask and not be guilty of a crime, but since Bragsworth has gone missing, the robberies have stopped."

"Meaning?"

"That he probably left of his own volition."

"So he had enough jewels for now so he moved on?"

"Exactly!"

"And leave his widow, Eunice, behind?"

"It's known to happen."

"Highly unlikely. I don't know the reason Bragsworth went missing, but there has to be a reason other than he just moved on. I can feel it."

"Can you feel how likely you'll be in jail tonight if you don't back off?"

I opened my mouth, but clamped it closed again. El's eyes pled with me to keep quiet and what other choice did I have but to comply with what the sheriff said. I had been in jail once before and that was more than enough.

We dragged our feet to the door and left just as forensics arrived. Maybe they can figure out what happened to Bridgett. If it was up to the sheriff, he'd file this one away as suicide, something I was sure wasn't the case. I just hoped I could prove that.

***

Back in my room, Eleanor was in the shower and Martha was still sleeping. Andrew had left a while before to check on Frank and Dorothy Alton, after much prodding on my part. I just wanted to make sure one of them hadn't kicked the bucket. Since their reunion they were behaving like newlyweds. Not that it's a bad thing, but it just creeps me out. Maybe these days Frank keeps his hearing aid turned up.

Eleanor surfaced from the bathroom, a steam trail in her wake. She was dressed in a Hawaiian print one-piece bathing suit.

"Where are you going, El?"

"Martha told me about this killer beach on the outskirts of town. It sounds marvy."

"You're still red from the last time."

She snickered. "I'm not going swimming, dear. I'm going sightseeing." She slipped on a pair of Jessica Simpson sunglasses and grabbed a camera from her bag. She turned just as a sleepy Martha appeared from the bedroom.

Martha waved as she made her way into the bathroom and closed the door. Next the shower cut on and I stood there with my foot tapping. "Where on earth is this beach?"

"Beats me, but it's one humdinger of a beach," she pouted. "Don't ruin this for me. I want to see some eye candy. The last time, we weren't at the beach long enough to enjoy the sights."

Sights, she says. I can't imagine what was in store for us next if Martha was running the show. Lord knows the last time Martha was in full swing, it was at a male stripper show. El ruined that one, thankfully, before I was given a lap dance at least. I can't imagine what's wrong with women these days. Nearly naked men don't do it for me. I'd rather reserve that honor for my brief encounters with Andrew.

The water cut off and Martha bolted out wearing a hot pink bikini. I hope they don't expect me to go along.

"Hurry, Aggie, before she leaves us behind."

"I'm not hurrying a bit. I'm not going. You two kids go ahead and have your fun. I'd rather wait for Andrew. We haven't even had much time to spend together, what with all the goings on around here of late. Plus, I wanted to find out if Peterson will tell me where the airport is where we first landed."

"He's not going to supply you with the info. And besides, his hands are full with filling out reports about Bridgett's suicide."

I raised a brow. "It wasn't a suicide."

"Prove it then."

"I can't if I'm forced to traipse around with you gals all day. We have us a mystery to solve, unless you have forgotten."

El stuck her tongue out at me. "No. I haven't forgotten, but Aggie I swear you won't want to miss this beach. I hear it's all the rage here in Florida."

I frowned, wondering just what in the hay El was talking about now. I can't believe this beach would be much different than the last.

Eleanor took out a beach bag and loaded it with sunscreen, towels and a blanket. Martha's mouth curved into a smile. What were these girls up to? No sense worrying about it. I had better go along to keep them out of trouble. I added my bathing suit to the bag, but I had no intention of going near the water. I'd just admire the pristine beach from afar.

Martha nudged El in the ribs. "Ready champ?"

"Champ, eh?"

"Relax Mom. You don't have to give yourself a stroke. The problem with you is that you never just let go and really relax. A massage couldn't hurt either. I know of a massage parlor downtown that does wonders."

"Massage parlor? The only ones that go to a massage parlor are horny men. It's hardly a place for respectable women to go."

"Get your mind out of the gutter. You need to replace the batteries in your lipstick thingy Eleanor told me about. What a hoot."

I glared at Eleanor. Of all the nerve, her sharing personal information *like that* with my daughter! I had long ago forgotten where I had put my personal massager. In the garbage, hopefully.

"I'm sure you misunderstood Eleanor."

"Whatever, Mom. Let's go already. You don't have to get all Mommie Dearest on me."

I had a mind to find a metal hanger and wrap it around my smart mouthed daughter's neck. *Calm down Agnes. She's just trying to ruffle your feathers.*

We clamored out the door and left via a taxi. When Martha rattled off the direction, the cab driver laughed. "Are you sure you want to go there. You're all so—"

Eleanor leaned forward. "Were you going to say old?"

"Of course not. It's just that I hope you brought

plenty of sunscreen is all."

Plenty of sunscreen? Where on earth was she taking us and why wouldn't El and Martha quit giggling like schoolgirls? I glared at them, but that only inspired them to laugh all the harder. Why did I feel like I was a lamb being led to the slaughter? If that Martha had her way, she'd find a way to humiliate me, although I had no clue why she'd care to do so.

Twenty minutes later the cab driver made a hard right and dropped us off. The water was calm today without a wave in sight. Was that the reason Martha wanted us to come to this beach? Were there baby sea turtles hatching?

We walked straight ahead and Martha and Eleanor dropped their bags with cameras in hand. I looked out to the ocean, but I didn't see anything until I whirled to the sound of Eleanor ooh-ing and ah-ing as she clicked away with her camera. My eyes widened. Everyone beside us was buck ass naked! Damn Martha and Eleanor had taken us to a nude beach!

I put a hand over my eyes as a man approached me. "You must be a newbie. You can just strip right here."

"I will do no such a thing."

Martha laughed, nearly choking on her tongue. "You're barking up the wrong tree, buddy. My mother still gets dressed in the dark."

I opened my eyes to snap a retort and that was when the man turned his cheeks to us. His muscled buttocks at that! When I finally glanced around I noticed most of the beach goers were of the younger sect with a group of senior citizens huddled under a large, striped umbrella, obviously too fair skinned to risk a direct hit from the UV rays.

I finally found my tongue. "Of all the outrageous things you have done, El, taking me to a nude beach is one of the worse."

"Oh, relax. Nobody says you have to join the natives and I don't plan to either. Martha on the other hand..."

Sure enough my daughter was taking her tiny bikini off even though I bellowed, "Stop it, Martha." I slapped a hand over my eyes. "I'd rather not have that image burned into the back of my eyes!"

From between spread fingers I noticed that Martha had spread a blanket on the beach and laid down. "I'm gonna soak up the rays. Yes, I am."

"You're gonna catch something."

Several sunbathers glanced in my direction, their eyes concealed behind large sunglasses.

I sat and whispered to Martha, "Don't say I didn't warn you."

Martha was enjoying herself as was Eleanor, who walked over to stand under the striped umbrella. Geez! I trudged through the thick sand before Eleanor got herself into any trouble.

"Eleanor! Come back here."

"That's my partner," she told the crowd. "She's always trying to boss me."

"I am not, but we need to leave. Isn't it time to take your medication?"

Eleanor glanced down at the man she was standing next to who was in his seventies from the looks of it. "The doctor said I need vitamin D. Well, there's no better source than the sun." With that the sky opened up and rain pounded the sand at our feet. Beachgoers ran for cover and soon we were surrounded by sweaty, tan naked bodies.

"Please God, don't blame Eleanor. She knows not what she does. All she wanted to do was see a few little buff bodies and now we are overcome with them."

Laughter surrounded us and we were offered sandwiches that Martha and Eleanor took, whereas I did not. I mean, where did these people go to wash their hands?

"Where do you ladies live?" a portly woman asked.

"In Michigan."

"I'm sure they have nude beaches in Michigan. It shouldn't be such a shock to you."

"We're not like that and I live near Lake Huron. We're just different there."

Eleanor elbowed me. "Uptight comes to mind."

I rolled my eyes. "Have Martha and you had enough fun for the day? Because I'm leaving."

I walked away in a huff. Even though the rain was pounding me silly, I kept moving. If I had to, I'd walk back to Sunny Brooke.

"Stop, Agnes. We don't have a car here, you know."

"In all my days, this is the worst thing you have ever done to me. You could have at least warned me."

"Then you wouldn't have come. It was great to see that horrified expression on your face. Life is too short to be so uptight, old girl. We're here to have fun. Let loose once in awhile."

I stood there bombarded with rain and an upset Martha ran to meet us. "They said they'll give us a lift back."

"Who?"

The naked group that consisted of seven senior citizens walked toward us and directed us to their bus with the word Anglewood Retirement Village emblazoned on the side. Once inside, the bus door closed and it rumbled back into town. Luckily enough, they dressed. What kind of town was this with nude beaches, a jewelry thief, counterfeiters, and missing persons, not to mention a possible suicide? So far, my trip to Florida was a complete bust. I could only imagine what tomorrow would bring.

Chapter Twenty

I awoke the next morning with a crick in my neck. After we had gotten home from the beach, we called it a day. It had rained the whole day and long into the night. Martha and Eleanor avoided me so far this morning, which should worry me after the events of yesterday. I still couldn't quite grasp why they had insisted on dragging me to a nude beach.

I dressed respectably today in a tan button up shirt and matching crop pants with ballerina flats. I hoped that the weather would at least have cleared up. I just hate being cooped up with nothing to do. Not much I could do investigation-wise with pending results of Bridgett's autopsy and I doubted Sheriff Peterson would be forthcoming. He seemed pretty stuck on the suicide theory.

Darcy had dropped off a pot of coffee, as I didn't feel up to journeying to the dining room. Sweet woman even brought me some vanilla flavored creamer.

Eleanor crossed the room to where I sat near the patio. "Okay. I'm sorry. Will you talk to me now?"

"I'm talking to you, but you haven't said a word to me all day. Where is your partner in crime, Martha?"

Hands flew to hips as El retorted, "She's not my partner in crime. You are!"

I sipped my coffee and set it down. "I'm willing to overlook what you two did yesterday if you promise to quit taking me places where naked people are."

"You willingly went to that stripper show."

"I know, but it wasn't supposed to be the full Monty."

Eleanor poured herself a cup of coffee. "I know, but what can I say—"

"That you're incorrigible, that you can't help yourself, that you don't know when to stop."

Eleanor took a sip and wrinkled her nose at the strong brew. "I don't know what to say, but I am sorry."

"Fine, just use some restraint the next time you feel impulsive."

Eleanor set her cup down with a thump. "You need to live a little, Aggie. I'm older than you are. If I don't have a little fun now, then when? Who knows what's around the corner. I could be laid up with a bad knee or something."

"Or have a bad hip like I have."

"And how does that work out when you're in the sack with Andrew?"

My face tightened. "You just never mind. How about Wilson?"

"I guess neither of us needs to be sharing those kinds of details. It might just give you nightmares."

I nodded and then cracked a smile. "So what's new downstairs today?"

"Oh, I don't know. Something about the owner visiting. He's Bridgett's dad, John. Word has it there's going to be a meeting in the commons room about three. All the residents are asked to attend."

I had a brainstorm. "Maybe he's going to give everyone back their deposit money."

"Humph. I'll believe that when I see it. These big city types like to stick together."

"I imagine he's upset about his daughter's death."

"But not too upset to plan a meeting so soon," El gasped.

"Well, life does go on. I suppose it wouldn't kill us to do some cleaning until then. I'd hate to be tossed out for not living up to the deal that bonehead sheriff made back home."

We finished our coffee and located our housekeeping carts, making a room-by-room sweep. It's not what I'd call the best cleaning job, but it would make do. We even found out that Eunice had relocated to the second floor, but she had the do not disturb sign hanging so no such luck checking out her room.

Promptly at three o'clock, we were in the commons room like the rest of the residents. In strode a portly man dressed in khaki shorts and shirt. He had white hair with round spectacles that rested on his pickle-sized nose!

"Thanks for attending this meeting. I'm John Nelson, Bridgett's father, and owner of this retirement village."

Jack Winston sat across from us and bellowed, "So you're the one who was trying to swindle us."

John didn't react in the slightest. "Nobody is trying to swindle anyone. We're just running a business here."

Sweat beaded up and dripped down Jack's nose.

"Where's the swimming pool from the brochure then, in the swamp?"

"I'm not sure what brochure you are referring to."

Jack promptly placed one in John's hands. He

skimmed it and then said, "I'm sorry for the mistake. This is the Anglewood Retirement Village's brochure. I'm not sure how this got mixed up."

Anglewood, as in naked seniors at the beach, I snickered to myself with an amused Eleanor looking on.

Jack pounded his fist on the pool table he was sitting at. "I want a refund of the deposit money so I can move somewhere else."

"In the middle of the season? I don't think you'll find suitable accommodations in the state of Florida at this late date, unless of course, you plan to go back home. Where do you live?"

"In Michigan."

"Brrr. I bet it's pretty cold back there about now. It's much nicer here."

I raised my hand. "Then what do you plan to do about the deposits paid by the residents?"

"Nothing. It's part of the lease, Ms.—what's your name, dear?"

"Agnes, Agnes Barton, super sleuth."

His brow furrowed. "Oh, yes. I believe my daughter told me about you. Have you solved the missing persons' cases yet?"

"No."

"Well, then, you better get busy, dear," he winked, "before another mishap occurs on your watch."

My watch? "Mishap? Please explain yourself."

"Well, Eugene Bragsworth has gone missing and then my daughter's murder."

"Murder? But the sheriff told us it was suicide."

"I don't much care for what old Peterson says. I

know my daughter wouldn't just up and hang herself."

"He claims it was because of the money that was stolen from me."

"You needn't go on about that. I'm well aware of what my daughter was accused of, but it's simply not true. Bridgett couldn't lie if she tried."

"And the mix up with the brochures would be whose fault then?"

"I'm not here to hash this all up. I just want to assure everyone that it will be business as usual around here. All lease agreements will be upheld."

I just had to know. "And who will be here to make sure things run smoothly?"

His smile faded. "I will, until I can hire another manager."

He said that like he had hired his own daughter. Something about this man bugged me, but I couldn't put my finger on it. Business as usual, indeed. He's as crooked as his daughter was.

"Please go back to your routine schedules everyone. I'm sure things will be cleared up about the missing money. Perhaps somebody will turn it in."

I about choked on my tongue. Turn it in indeed. My eyes narrowed as John pranced back into the other room.

"Well, he certainly is of the same cloth," Eleanor spat. "I have half of a mind to check up on him. Nobody is that cheerful after his daughter just died."

"I agree with you there, but not much else we can do. Who would we even ask about him that would tell us anything?"

"Edith Stone sure seemed nice. I bet she'd be happy

to help."

"Are you talking about the sheriff's mother?"

"Yes."

I frowned. "How would we even find out where she lives?"

"I know where she lives," a woman beside us said.

"Please, do tell."

"She lives on Baker Street. She owns a bakery there, Sweet Confections."

***

An hour later, we were at the front door of Sweet Confections. The name was etched on the glass door, and as we walked through the door, a bell rang. A dark haired girl surfaced via a door that was located behind a glass-cased counter. She wiped her hands on her white apron, which was stained with pink frosting. "Can I help you, ladies?"

Eleanor flew to the counter, eyeing the delicious goodies that consisted of donuts, cakes, and cup cakes.

"Yes, we're here to see Edith Stone if she's available."

"Sure thing." She whirled into the back and Edith appeared a few minutes later, dressed all in white, a hairnet on her silver hair.

"Why, hello there, Agnes. What can I do for you?"

Eleanor smiled widely. "I'd love a glazed donut for one."

Edith took the requested donut out with a sheer paper and handed it to Eleanor, who was digging in her big black monstrosity of a purse. She took out her pink pistol, setting it on the counter and then retrieved her coin purse counting out the cost of the donut."

Edith smiled. "I hope this isn't a hold up."

"Eleanor, put that blasted gun away. I'm sorry, Edith."

Eleanor tucked the pistol away. "Sorry."

"It's quite all right. I have my own pistol behind the counter. It's a Pink Lady by Charter Arms." She pulled it out for us to inspect.

"We have one of those at home, but I had to buy this one here. It's not very wise to bring one on a plane. I'd hate to be arrested. Back at home we have a concealed weapons permit."

"Me, too," Edith said with a wink. "I feel safer having my trusted girl here."

Eleanor bit into her donut and asked, "Have you ever been robbed?"

"No and I hope it stays that way. At least the jewelry store robberies have stopped."

Thanks to Bragsworth's disappearance no doubt. "That's good, but I'm afraid the woman running Sunny Brooke was found dead."

"I heard about Bridgett. That's awful. I bet John is going out of his mind now."

"How's that?"

"Well, he has been trying to retire for years, but Sunny Brooke has been taking up all his time. He recently turned over the reins to Bridgett, but with her gone—"

"He told us it was business as usual. He didn't even seem upset his daughter supposedly killed herself."

"Suicide? I think not. Bridgett is too greedy for that.

Sunny Brooke was her cash cow. I believe she thought her dad would soon be signing over the place to her."

She totally dodged my question about John. "And about John not being upset?"

"I'm sure he is, but truthfully his granddaughter, Isabella, is the apple of his eye. He's been disappointed with Bridgett for many years. Everything he has given her she turned to muck, but she seemed to really turn things around at Sunny Brooke. The last few years she has had a full house, even with a swamp is in the backyard."

"It's surprising that she hasn't lost residents over that one."

"About five couples left last season, but she managed to fill their slots. This is a pretty popular destination for northern transplants."

"Transplants?"

"I mean you northern folks looking to escape the snow and ice."

"This is my first winter in Florida and it is rather nice, if not for all the crime."

Eleanor licked her lips. "Finding Bridgett like that wasn't fun either."

Edith leaned over the counter. "So how did she do it? I promise I won't tell a soul."

"She hung herself," Eleanor informed her. "Just awful."

"It's unclear to me if it was suicide or murder. I can't go into details though."

"Nope," El smacked her lips. "We're senior snoops. Plus, your son would get awful mad if we told you more. He seems to believe she committed suicide."

"I don't believe it is all I can say."

I grabbed a napkin for Eleanor. "How well do you know John?"

"Very well. He's a social butterfly, but he's been downstate for the last few months."

"Do you consider him an upstanding man?"

"Yes, but I'm not sure what you mean?"

"Is he the type to use trickery to fill Sunny Brooke?"

She gasped. "Well, no." She shook her head. "I can't see him doing anything like that at all."

I headed for the door. "Thanks for your help."

"Anytime. I'm sure you'll figure out the truth, Agnes."

"Hey, what am I, chopped liver?" Eleanor spat. "I'm her sidekick, don't ya know?"

She laughed. "Of course, Eleanor. I'd never count you out. Just be careful both of you. I'd hate to lose two such great investigators."

We wandered outside and sat on a bench near the door. "She made John sound like a saint, but his reaction to his daughter's death is way off for me. I'm not sure if I'm buying the idea that he had no clue about how the wrong brochure was being used."

Eleanor began making her observations. "If what Edith said was true, he was disappointed with Bridgett, but she turned the business around. For once in her life she did something right."

She had a point. "Okay."

"She did some unscrupulous things to get that place going. If five couples left last year, I wonder how many left this year?"

"Good question, El. She made herself a tidy sum last year. Maybe that's why she stole our money. With no couples leaving early this year—"

"There'd be no extra cash to take, but her death sure throws a wrench in the plan."

I rubbed my neck. "True. There has to be a reason she was offed, but what?"

El's face lit up. "Maybe she knew who stole our money and she was trying to cover it up. What if she was planning to tell the sheriff the whole story, and somebody killed her to hush her up."

"That, or they worried she'd go to the police."

Eleanor pulled up the strap of her purse. "So we have another suspect to find."

"Or suspects. We still have the disappearances of three people."

"And the jewelry thief is still at large."

"But Bragsworth—"

El slapped her legs. "We don't know he was responsible for the robberies. It could be somebody else."

"Unless he decided to quit. What if his whole disappearance is a ruse? He might have just taken off before he got caught."

"Thieves can't quit. It's never enough for them. He might pick up and leave town, but he can't quit."

"What if the same jewelry thief is responsible for stealing the money?"

"That would give him plenty of money to take off with. Maybe he plans to move his operation."

I glanced down the street, spying a pawnshop. "Either way, he's one greedy person. We need to find out if any of the jewels have been hocked or pawned."

We stood and made our way to a pawnshop named Strapped Cash. We wandered past the barred windows and inside, making our way around lawn mowers and furniture to a counter where a bald man was looking through a small eyeglass at a diamond ring. He stopped at our approach.

"Hello, ladies. Are you buying or pawning."

"Neither," I said. "We're looking for information."

"I don't give away information. I do sell it though."

I pulled out a twenty and slid the bill to the man."

"You're killing me here. I need more than a twenty. How about a fifty."

"How about you answering one question first?"

He waved his hands in the air. "Fine, one."

"Has anyone tried to pawn any of the jewelry that was stolen in the jewelry store robberies?"

His eyes bulged slightly. "Slide me another thirty and I'll tell you."

Eleanor opened her bag and came back with the extra thirty.

"And where did you get your money from? I thought the purse thief stole all your money that you had in your purse."

She gasped. "Well, I expect from the same place you got your money, from Andrew."

"So he loaned you money, too. That was awful nice of him."

"Loaned? You sure have an odd relationship with that man of yours."

"I don't need a man for money. They have a word for women like that."

"Yes, happy."

He eyed us with a raised brow as we went on like he wasn't even there. He took the money, counting it. "I don't buy stolen merchandise. I'm on the up and up, but I had a piece someone tried to pawn. I called the sheriff, but she didn't stick around long enough."

A woman? "She was gone before the sheriff got here?"

"Yes."

"It was a woman, not a man then?"

"Yes, and she was alone."

"What did she look like?"

"She was about your age with salt and pepper hair. I was surprised a woman her age would be trying to fence jewelry, but who knows. I wish I had asked her for her ID when she came in with her far-fetched story."

"What was her story?"

"That her husband bought her the necklace, but she didn't like it and the jewelry store wouldn't take it back."

"She might not have known it was stolen."

"No, but she sure lit outta here. She even left the necklace behind."

"That is odd. You'd have thought she would have known better to try and pawn a stolen piece of jewelry like that."

He nodded. "Yeah, but I have seen all kinds in this business."

"I imagine you have. Do you have any surveillance equipment, like maybe a camera that captured her image?"

He clammed up just then, staring down at the money as if contemplating asking for more. "Yes, I suppose I could give you a peek, but isn't this official police business? I'd hate for the sheriff to find out I told you something I shouldn't have."

Official police business. Here we go again. "The sheriff knows I'm working this case. He won't mind if we just take a peek."

"He won't, eh? You two must be amateur sleuths. If you were working the case with Peterson, you'd already know what I'm about to show you, but I'm in a generous mood so I'll go fetch the picture. The sheriff took all the surveillance discs. I like to keep my own copies, though, just in case they lose them. Stranger things have happened in this town."

Yeah, like too many crimes to count. "Thanks for your help."

He went into the back and came back with a color photo of a woman who wore a white, large rimmed floppy hat and dark sunglasses. Sure enough her hair was salt and pepper, but she was looking down the whole time like she didn't want to be identified. I thought I recognized her, too. It was—

"That's Eunice Bragsworth!" El bellowed.

"You sure ripped that outta my mouth, El."

"You're sure?" the man said.

"Positive. Call the sheriff with our findings. We'll try to nab the perp before she leaves town. I can't imagine she'll stay it town any longer. She knows someone is on to her."

We left the shop in a hurry and headed to the corner where the Sunny Brooke's bus sat. Darcy opened the door and we rumbled aboard.

"Did you get all your errands run?" she asked, noting that we carried no packages.

I was shaking inside. "We sure did. Thanks for driving us."

"Not a problem. It feels great to get out of the kitchen."

I made small talk to try and still my irregular breathing pattern. "Who's cooking, then?"

"I made vegetable lasagna. All Mr. Wilson had to do was turn the oven on. That shouldn't be too difficult to remember."

I hope she knows she's talking about a senior citizen here, one who might barely remember five minutes ago.

Chapter Twenty-One

El and I huddled in the back of the bus. "So, El, it looks like ole Bragsworth was the jewelry thief, just like we thought."

"I still think somebody else is involved. He's missing, remember?"

"I know. I think his wife Eunice offed him and then made off with the jewelry."

"No, I'm certain somebody else might be involved. I just don't see Bragsworth capable of accessing our lockers."

"Bridgett might have done that."

"We have already been through this. She was killed to shut her up. Somebody else was involved. I can feel it."

The bus screeched to a stop and El and I scrambled from the bus. We raced past a bemused Jessica and made our way toward Bragsworth's room, when Frank Alton ran from the commons room. "Help! Somebody has kidnapped my wife. Dorothy is missing!"

I grabbed Frank's shoulders. "Are you sure? When was the last time you saw her?"

"She went upstairs to take a nap and never returned. When I came to the room, she was gone."

I released Frank. This certainly was a strange turn of events until I remembered how Bragsworth had been eyeing Dorothy's jewels. "I think I might know where she is."

"But, Agnes, her shoes were by the swamp."

"That's a ruse. Nobody has ever been eaten by alligators unless after the fact. They have all been murdered."

One lone tear trickled down Frank's wrinkled face. "Don't say that."

I grabbed ahold of Frank's shirt. "Come on. Let's get Dorothy back."

We raced to the elevator and climbed in once it stopped, pounding the number two button. It slowly rose to the second floor and we ran toward Bragsworth's room. I pounded on the door until a sheepish Eunice answered the door.

I pushed the door open slightly. "We're here to get Dorothy. We know she's in there!"

"Very well. You have found me out, my persistent investigator. But in my defense I only wanted to get back at her for trying to steal my husband."

The door was opened and a frantic Dorothy sat trussed to a chair, a gag stuffed into her mouth. "You let her go!" Eleanor shouted.

Frank ran to his wife's side and pulled at the ropes. "Don't worry, dear. It will be okay. I'm here to save you."

Eunice clucked her tongue. "Are you now?"

"Yes, I am," he stomped his foot.

She pulled out a pistol and snatched Eleanor's purse away. Pointing the gun at me now, she bellowed, "Hand over your purse," pointing at El, "or I'll shoot your friend."

What choice did I have? But I planned to smack her

with it.

"Set it down now. I'm not stupid enough to let you hit me with the bag. I wasn't born yesterday."

I laid my purse on the floor and kicked it to her with a bit of force, but she never even blinked an eye. "Good move. Now get over there with your friends."

We huddled together and I then asked, "Where is your accomplice, Ernie Bragsworth?"

"You mean Eugene don't you." She laughed. "You didn't really think that he had a real twin that looks just like him did you?"

"No, I didn't, but where is he now?"

"Downtown about now. He was arrested in town not long ago."

I bided my time until the sheriff showed up. "He tried to rob another jewelry store?"

Eunice's lips contorted into a sinister laugh. "Oh, please. Eugene couldn't rob anyone. He's too chicken livered. He's a cad, but not up for a robbery."

If Bragsworth wasn't the jewelry thief, then who was?

"You're stumped aren't you?" she snickered.

There was a hurried knock at the door and when the door opened, Jamie Odell, the maintenance man stood there with a suitcase. His eyes widened at the four of us. "I told you to kill her and be done with it, and now you have three more witnesses to off."

I gulped at that. "So you're the jewelry thief! I should have guessed it. You fit the body type perfectly."

"Yes," he sneered. "And I tried to off you two in town, but I missed. I just hate snoopy old bats."

I squared my shoulders. “I know. El and I are a criminal’s worse enemy.”

El took a step forward. “Yeah. Back off, buddy. We’re all leaving here.”

“In a body bag is the only way you’re leaving.”

El gulped and fell silent.

“So you were also the one who stole our purses and money.”

“Yeah, so what if I was?”

“Bridgett found out, didn’t she, and that’s why you killed her.”

“She knew the whole time. You really messed up a good thing. When residents left before their leases were up, Bridgett pocketed the money and gave me a share, but this year nobody left, and I was forced to scrounge up money any way I could. I couldn’t believe my luck in finding twenty-five thousand in your purse, but Bridgett found out and went ballistic. You two had her running scared. I thought when I pitched your purses in town it would smooth things over, that the sheriff would look elsewhere, but no go. He immediately thought Bridgett was responsible. Killing her was the only way to assure she’d keep her trap shut. I set it up as a suicide. You should give me points on setting that one up. Even the sheriff believed it was a suicide.”

My hands flew to my hips. “I never believed it for a minute and the sheriff would have known too when the autopsy report came back.”

Jamie rubbed his chin in thought. “Maybe. I should have offed you two early on. If only the bullets hadn’t missed.”

“So what about the ski mask found in Bragsworth’s

room? You planted it, didn't you?"

"Yes. I figured the sheriff would think when Bragsworth went missing, that he left town. He'd do a search elsewhere that way."

"Then why the ruse of Bragsworth's twin brother?"

"That was her doing." He turned to Eunice. "I told you that was a bad idea."

"If it wasn't for him, you or I'd be in jail right now."

Jamie clenched his fist. "Why was he arrested?"

"Because the money you stole from them was counterfeit!"

I had an aha moment. "So you went with him when he spent the money?"

"Yes. He was supposed to buy us plane tickets, but the fuzz was on him quicker than a bear on honey."

"What about the maids? Who killed them?"

Jamie went face-to-face with me. "I have been robbing jewelry stores for awhile. Those maids found a ski mask and stolen jewelry in my tool box and I had to kill them. I dumped their bodies in the swamp out back. Bridgett helped spread the alligator theory and the sheriff seemed to agree until you two snoopy old hags starting pressing him." Jamie's face reddened. "Killing you is going to be a great feeling. You screwed me out of twenty-five thousand. Where did you get all that counterfeit cash anyway?"

I backed up. "I-I found it."

"Where?"

"On an airplane. I found it by default."

"If not for your hoax I would have left town much earlier. I should have killed you during the jewelry store robbery."

"Stop it, Jamie," Eunice said. "We need to get out of here before somebody finds us."

"Yeah, the sheriff is coming," Eleanor said.

I nudged her in the ribs and said between gritted teeth. "Stop it El, before they kill us."

"Let me see your gun for a minute," he said to Eunice who handed it over. "Good, now get over with them. This is how it's going to go. I'm going to kill them all with your gun and then use mine to kill you. I'll look very heroic, don't you think?"

"You dumb ass. I helped you and this is how it goes? You said you loved me."

"Loved you?" he spat. "You're an old bat. I was just using you. How else was I going to make people think Bragsworth was no good? But you had your own motives. You were trying to cozy up with Frank for his money. We were supposed to be a team. I don't trust you as far as I can throw you."

Jamie untied Dorothy who ran to Frank giving him butterfly kisses. "Get moving out the door, now!" Jamie spat.

El and I went through the door first, followed by Frank and Dorothy. It was then that I noticed Mr. Wilson. He stood next to the door, holding his walker like a samurai sword. Eunice came through the door next and then Jamie. "Whoosh." Mr. Wilson slammed down the walker, knocking the gun from Jamie's hand. It thumped to the floor and there was a mad scramble for the gun, but Eunice came back with it and fired the gun, striking Jamie in the chest. We scattered, making way for the elevator and narrowly made it inside with the doors closed.

"Where is Wilson?" screamed El. It was then that I realized he wasn't with us. "Oh God, my poor baby is dead!"

"We can't do anything about it now, El."

"He can't walk without his walker. He's helpless!"

I have seen Wilson in action before like with Eleanor, and he was anything but helpless. "Don't worry, El. We'll go back for him when the sheriff arrives."

The elevator door opened and the sheriff had arrived with Putner and Palmer from Homeland Security! We rushed forward and that's when we heard a scream from the stairs. Eunice had her gun pointed directly at us. Guns were drawn and a surprised Eunice let her gun fall, but it went off, striking Eleanor in the thigh. She screamed as she went down and I raced to her side placing a hand over her wound, trying to staunch the flow of blood. "Please, somebody check on Mr. Wilson. We had to leave him upstairs," I cried. "Eunice shot the maintenance man, Jamie Odell. "I'm so sorry, Eleanor."

Her bottom lip trembled. "I-It's okay."

Footsteps pounded up the stairs and I glanced up and looked into the eyes of Mr. Hawk Nose. I gasped as did El, until he raised his hands. "Would you two please quit? I'm Stephen Knight from Secret Service."

We both sighed in relief, but even more so when the elevator doors opened and Mr. Wilson rolled forward, luckily unharmed.

He made way for Eleanor. "Oh, Peaches! My poor Peaches got shot."

"It was an accident," she cried. "It's only a f-flesh wound."

"And lucky for you that you have plenty of flesh," I said with a tear in my eye. "I wish I was the one hit. I'd hate to lose a friend like you. You were so right about a different accomplice."

"We both were shocked to learn how tangled this case was. Who knew the maintenance man was the culprit all along?"

"Or that Eunice was in love with Jamie."

El nodded. "People do stranger things for love."

I turned my attention back to Stephen Knight. "So why would someone from Secret Service kill a pilot?"

"We didn't kill him. We used a stun gun on him. The pilot was transporting counterfeit money."

"But Sheriff Clem Peterson back home hired him."

"He didn't know he was on the Homeland Security watch list."

"Did the sheriff call you boys down here?"

"No, we came here to question you once more after Bragsworth was arrested. We thought you were trying to dupe us."

"Why didn't Putner and Palmer tell us what was going on? They kept talking about a packet, but wouldn't tell us what was in it."

"The investigation was kept quiet until we found enough evidence."

"If I had known, I would have told them I found twenty-five thousand in cash, but obviously it was counterfeit money the whole time, right?"

"Yes, if it was the same money Eugene Bragsworth tried to use to purchase airplane tickets."

"I just think they should have told us, is all. I'd have told them if I had known. Did you recover all of the counterfeit money?"

"Yes, Bragsworth had it all. He's currently in jail and now we have enough evidence to charge the pilot from the airplane.

"Eunice used Bragsworth to pass the money. None of them knew the money was counterfeit, but that was his only crime. He wasn't responsible for the jewelry robberies. Jamie Odell was. I don't think he knew about the money scheme the retirement home was doing or that his wife was guilty as an accessory. She was also the one who tried to pawn some of the jewelry at a pawn shop."

Peterson surfaced and said, "Thanks for having the pawn shop call me."

"No, thank you for coming so quickly." I frowned. "Did someone call an ambulance yet?"

Sheriff Peterson said, "Yes. Your boyfriend, Andrew Hart, went to check out the swamps in case you wonder where he is."

"And why is he there?"

"He went there to look for Dorothy Alton who was reported missing."

"Well, somebody get my Andrew out of the swamp before he gets eaten by a gator."

Peterson swirled a finger and two deputies ran out back.

Epilogue

Where are the chicken fingers I ordered?" El asked from her hospital bed.

"I'm sure they'll be here soon," I pacified Eleanor.

She motioned to her bandaged thigh. "Easy for you to say. I'm the one trussed up like a turkey."

"Oh, El. I'm still so sorry you were hit. I guess Andrew was right about this investigative stuff. It sure is dangerous."

From a bedside chair, Andrew added, "You admit I'm right about that at last."

"Yes, and I guess it wouldn't hurt to take a break."

He laughed. "I'll believe that when I see it."

Sheriff Clem Peterson smiled from the other side of Eleanor's bed. "I'm so sorry about the pilot. I had no idea he was a crook, but I must admit I was the one who sent you to Sunny Brooke to solve the *case of the missing maids*."

"Huh? That sounds like a great title for a mystery novel."

"It sure does. I'm looking forward to the time my two favorite senior snoops return to Michigan."

I laughed. "You were that bored with us gone, eh?"

He scratched his head. "Sure, but that doesn't mean that I won't give you a hard time the next time you butt into one of my cases."

"I'd expect no less from you. So how is Trooper

Sales these days?"

"Why don't you ask him yourself?" With that, Trooper Sales walked in with my granddaughter, Sophia, close to his side.

Martha walked in crying. "My baby is going to have a baby."

My eyes narrowed and Andrew held me down before I could—

There was no sense making waves about something that could be saved for another day though. Plenty of time to worry about that and shotgun weddings later once we were back in Michigan. Lucky for El and me, we'd both be around for yet another case another day.

Author Bio

When independent writer Madison Johns began writing at the age of forty-four, she never imagined she'd have two books in her Agnes Barton Senior Sleuths mystery series make it onto the USA Today Bestsellers list. Sure, these books are Amazon bestsellers, but USA Today?

Although sleep-deprived from working third shift, she knew if she used what she had learned while caring for senior citizens to good use, it would result in something quite unique. The Agnes Barton Senior Sleuths mystery series has forever changed Madison's life, with each of the books making it onto the Amazon bestseller's list for cozy mystery and humor.

Madison is a member of Sisters In Crime. Madison is now able to do what she loves best and work from home as a full-time writer. She has two children, a black lab, and a hilarious Jackson Chameleon to keep her company while she churns out more Agnes Barton stories with a few others brewing in the pot.

Agnes Barton Senior Sleuths Mystery series in order:
Armed and Outrageous
Grannies, Guns and Ghosts
Senior Snoops
Trouble in Tawas
Treasure in Tawas

An Agnes Barton/Kimberly Steele Cozy Mystery Series
Pretty, Hip &Dead

Romance books:
Pretty and Pregnant novella featuring Kimberly Steele
Redneck Romance (Published by Tirgearr Publishing)

Madison is a member of Sisters In Crime.
http://madisonjohns.com/
Join Madison's mailing list.
https://www.facebook.com/MadisonJohnsAuthor/app_100265896690345

Made in the USA
Lexington, KY
23 May 2016